THE *Sapphire* CUTLASS

by SHARON GOSLING

SWITCH PRESS

THE SAPPHIRE CUTLASS IS PUBLISHED IN 2016 BY SWITCH PRESS,
A CAPSTONE IMPRINT
1710 ROE CREST DRIVE
NORTH MANKATO, MINNESOTA 56003
WWW.SWITCHPRESS.COM

FIRST PUBLISHED IN 2016 BY CURIOUS FOX,
AN IMPRINT OF CAPSTONE GLOBAL LIBRARY LIMITED,
264 BANBURY ROAD, OXFORD, OX2
REGISTERED COMPANY NUMBER 6695582
WWW.CURIOUS-FOX.COM

LIBRARY OF CONGRESS CATALOGING-IN-PUBLICATION DATA IS AVAILABLE ON
THE LIBRARY OF CONGRESS WEBSITE.

ISBN: 978-1-63079-041-7 (JACKETED PAPER OVER BOARD)
ISBN: 978-1-63079-042-4 (EBOOK)

SUMMARY:
DANGER AWAITS AS RÉMY AND THE RUBY AIRSHIP'S CREW TRAVEL DEEP
INTO THE INDIAN JUNGLE TO LEARN THE TRUTH BEHIND THE MYSTERIOUS
SAPPHIRE CUTLASS. WILL RÉMY CHOOSE BETWEEN HELPING HER FRIENDS OR
FINDING HER TWIN BROTHER?

DESIGNER:
KAY FRASER

COVER ILLUSTRATION:
LIAM PETERS

IMAGE CREDIT:
SHUTTERSTOCK © LYNEA

PRINTED IN CHINA.
092015 009214S16

In loving memory of Andy Sears, who always looked good in a green jacket.

{Chapter 1}

THE TIGER
AND THE BIRD

$\mathcal{T}$he jungle fell silent.

A sudden hush dropped over the verdant foliage as if someone had trapped it inside a glass jar. The birds huddled closer to their branches, concealing their bright jewel colors beneath the sun-dappled leaves. The chattering hordes of black and white monkeys deserted their overhead perches, carrying their cries — and their babies — with them until the echoes faded into the distance. Even the insects ceased to buzz and skitter. The searing hot air of midmorning became still and empty, a strange sense of expectancy hanging in it.

The chital froze and raised its head, the white dots

that peppered the little deer's reddish brown flanks quivering as it sniffed the air.

Rémy cursed silently. Crouched beneath a bush just a few feet away, she was hot, cramped, and tired of this hunt, which had been going on all morning without success. Whatever had scared the fawn at this crucial moment was in danger of depriving her of her dinner. The loop of rope that belonged to the makeshift trap she had set hours before lay just beyond where the creature now stood.

Go on, Rémy urged it silently. *Just a little farther . . .*

The chital turned, head still up, ears flicking this way and that, and took a step toward Rémy's hiding place. *No*, Rémy thought. *Not this way!*

The deer, oblivious and still afraid, took another step in the wrong direction. It looked as if it were preparing to bolt.

Sensing a last chance, Rémy stood, but the deer was already moving. It leapt toward her, its small but powerful back legs kicking up the dust of the forest floor. Rémy lunged forward, arms stretched wide as if she could herd the creature in the right direction, but the chital flicked sideways in midair, black eyes wide with fright, nostrils flaring.

If, in those briefest of moments, Rémy had time

to wonder why the deer had chosen to run *at* her rather than *away*, the question was swiftly answered. Something surged out of the undergrowth behind it, a flash of orange and white striped with black, massive and muscular with a gaping maw and yellowed teeth as large and sharp as carving knives. The huge creature sliced through the clearing, bathing Rémy in a wash of air that rolled over her as it passed.

The cat caught the chital, one massive bite from those fangs crushing the deer's neck before the beast rippled to a halt at the edge of the clearing, giant paws as silent as slippers on the jungle floor.

The tiger turned to look at Rémy Brunel.

The cat's head was enormous, almost half the size of the deer between its teeth. The tiger's body easily dwarfed Rémy's, and even now, from several feet away, she could see the rippling muscles beneath the bright beauty of its glossy tri-colored coat.

Blood dripped from the tiger's razor-sharp teeth, peppering the earth with scarlet. Nothing else moved. The tiger watched her with huge, sepia-colored eyes, as if waiting to see what she would do. Rémy herself didn't know. The tiger already had prey to occupy it, but the chital was small. She would make a bigger meal. If she moved, would it come after her? If it did,

Rémy knew that as swift as she was, she'd never out-run a tiger in full flight.

The Little Bird was no match at all for a Big Cat. Not on the ground, anyway . . .

The tiger twitched, lifting one huge front paw and setting it down again. She could see its claws, shining like opaque, slivered jewels through the feathery white fur of its feet.

The tiger growled, the muscles along its nose wrinkling like waves on the ocean, its whiskers quiver-ing. Rémy turned and ran. She made for the nearest tree, throwing herself at it and scrambling skyward up the parched bark at breakneck speed. She felt the tiger coming at her, its bulk disturbing the still air as it crossed the clearing in one leap. It thumped against the tree, shaking the trunk with its full weight so that Rémy almost lost her grip. She clung on, digging her nails into the bark, feeling it give under her fingers as she pulled herself up. The tiger leapt after her, paw outstretched and body extended, so big that she was sure she would feel its claws in her legs. Rémy kept going, scrambling higher and higher until she was out of the creature's reach. Breathing hard, she allowed herself a pause to look down.

The tiger was climbing the tree, using its needle-sharp claws to drag itself upward. It snarled, the sound dispersing like the low rumble of thunder through the trees.

Rémy ran quickly along the narrow branch, balancing even as the tiger's movements shook and shuddered it beneath her booted feet. It began to bow beneath her weight, but by then she had lined up a jump. Taking a fraction of a second to center herself, Rémy flung herself into midair, the colors of the jungle whipping past her like circus streamers as she reached for a branch of the neighboring tree. Her hands gripped and held the rough bark like the bar of a trapeze and she swung there for a moment, testing its strength. To her relief, it held. She bounced there for a second, then used the momentum to twist one hand over the other, turning to see what her hunter was doing.

The tiger snarled again and dropped back to the ground, too clever to follow her along the narrow branch. It moved to stand beneath her instead. Rémy hung there, nothing but the strength of her arms and several feet of empty, hot jungle air between her and the angry cat. It hunched itself backward on its hindquarters.

She swung out of the way as the tiger leapt, snapping its jaws around empty air. She hooked her legs over the branch and heaved herself onto her stomach, just as she would have done on the trapeze, then found her way to her feet. She moved higher, where the branches were thinner but out of the reach of the tiger's questing claws. Still the creature stood below her, those great yellow eyes watching every movement, just waiting for her to make a mistake.

Rémy, out of breath, realized that she'd have to take the monkey's highway if she wanted to escape in one piece. *It's just as well*, she thought as she scanned the trees around her for her next move, *that I have kept up my training, even though there has been no proper audience to watch me for months.*

She set off, zigzagging from branch to branch through the trees, hands protesting at the rough nature of the holds she reached for over and over again. The tiger padded along beneath her for a long way, snarling every now and then, waiting for her to make a mistake. Rémy Brunel, however, rarely made mistakes — at least, not on the trapeze. She climbed, she jumped, and she swung, as nimble and light as a bird — or a monkey.

Rémy didn't see the tiger go. One minute it was

there, following below her like a flash of orange flame. The next it had melted back into the jungle. Most likely it was returning to the clearing to reclaim the chital before a pack of dhole came across it.

Still, she stuck to the trees. Just in case.

Chapter 2

PUZZLES

$\mathcal{I}$t took Rémy more than an hour to get back to the airship. Her crew had set her down in a small clearing that housed an ornate ruined temple. Rémy had been reluctant to take the swiftest route in case the tiger followed her, and besides, she hadn't wanted to return empty-handed. As it was, when she finally walked into the camp, Rémy carried over her shoulder a brace of rabbits — not quite the venison of the chital, it was true, but at least there would be something for the pot that night.

"Rémy!" Dita's voice danced out of the trees toward her. She looked up, just in time to see the little girl jump down from the lowest branch of the nearest tree. "You've been ages! I thought you were lost!"

"Lost? Me? Never!" Rémy told her with a smile. "Just a little waylaid, that's all."

"I have been practicing," Dita said proudly, "while you were gone. I can almost get all the way to the end without falling now."

Rémy looked at the taut rope that she and Thaddeus had strung between the two sturdiest trees that edged the clearing. It was four feet from the ground and at least eight feet long. "That's very good indeed," she said, genuinely impressed, making a mental note to adjust her next few lessons to accommodate Dita's apparently natural skill on the wire. "Especially since you've only been learning for a few weeks."

"Well, it is *wichtig*," said Dita, who still had the habit of peppering her English with words from her native German language. Her face took on a solemn look. "When we return home to Europe, I want a proper circus job." She wrinkled her nose. "No more sweeping up after the messy elephants. If I can walk a rope, then I can do *anything*. Like you, *ja*?"

Rémy grinned, as much at the girl's enthusiasm as the compliment. "I'm not sure about *anything*," she said, pulling her catch from her shoulder and holding it up. "I'm still not too good at cooking."

"Pfft!" exclaimed Dita, her hands on her hips. "But

that is a good thing! It means the boys have to do it. They have to be useful for something!"

Rémy smiled again and then looked around. The clearing was very quiet. "Where are they, anyway?" she asked.

Dita nodded toward the silent airship, at rest between two crumbling yellow walls with its balloon fully inflated, which it hadn't been when Rémy left. "J, he is hard at work on the ruby mechanism," she said with a roll of her eyes. "He thinks it is not working quite as smoothly as it should. Honestly, even if there were nothing wrong with it, he would find something to tinker with. Boys with toys, *ja*?"

"What about Thaddeus?" Rémy asked, walking to the area that had been designated as their "kitchen" and dropping the rabbits in a heap beside the remnants of the previous night's fire.

"The other side," Dita said, indicating the airship again. She grinned wickedly. "He is an Englishman, no? He must hide from all this terrible sun!"

Rémy skipped quickly over a pile of fallen yellow wall, retrieved her bag from inside the airship, shouted a hello to the out-of-sight J, and went to find Thaddeus Rec. He was sitting in the dappled shadows cast by the dense forest behind him, a large map spread out over his knees and his old policeman's notebook and pencil in one hand. His feet were bare; his trousers rolled up to his calves. His white shirt, although clean, was looking somewhat worse for wear after months of travel and was pulled up to the elbows and open at the throat. Rémy paused to watch him for a moment, smiling at the look of utter concentration on his face. Thaddeus's skin had darkened to a rich bronze tan in the sun that had followed them ever since they had reached the coast of India.

"Afternoon, *Monsieur*," Rémy said softly as she approached. She knelt down beside him and kissed him on his cheek, which bore a prickle of dark stubble.

"Good afternoon, Miss Brunel," said Thaddeus, accepting the kiss with a smile. "I was beginning to wonder whether I should form a search party to come looking for you."

She shrugged with a grin, leaning against the tree beside him and stretching out her legs beneath the map. "This little bird had an encounter with a big cat."

Thaddeus raised his eyebrows. "Oh?"

"A tiger. A big one, too — much bigger than me."

"A tiger? Good grief — are you all right?" He looked horrified, and she laughed.

"I am fine, as you see. Though tonight I think we

should all sleep in the airship and seal the hatch. Just in case."

Thaddeus touched her cheek and nodded. "Good idea. I want to move on tomorrow, anyway — I don't like staying in one place for too long. It's too risky, with the airship."

Rémy glanced at the craft that had flown them all the way from Europe to the heart of England's colonial empire. They had been forced to dodge the curiosity of the British army a few times since they'd arrived, but that had mainly been near the coast, where their ships clustered in the teeming ports. Farther inland, beyond the big cities, they had seen fewer colonial uniforms.

"Surely here, in the jungle, it is safe?"

Thaddeus frowned. "Perhaps. But I just have this feeling that it's better to keep on the move. The airship would be a rich prize for anyone, and without it we would be completely stranded."

Rémy nodded. "True enough. So, where to next, then?" she asked, indicating the map. "What has it told you, *Monsieur* Englishman? What are you looking for?"

He sighed. "I know we said we'd steer as clear as we could of the palace J remembers from his visit with Desai last year, but I think we're going to have to try there next. The trail has led us in that direction any-way. We can't be more than twenty miles from it now."

Rémy traced her eyes over the map and his open notebook, which was full of the notes Thaddeus had kept throughout their journey. The airship had been in this clearing for the past three days as her crew tried to work out where to take her next. They had followed every lead they'd been given and it had brought them here, to this lush jungle that reached up from the coast southeast of them to cut a huge swathe through the center of the massive continent of India. Now the trail had run cold.

"Have you asked J what we can expect if we do go there?" she asked. "It would be good if we could pre-pare a little for what might greet us."

Thaddeus shook his head. "J says that Desai made the final journey to see the raja himself — he wouldn't let J or his friend Tommy accompany him."

Rémy frowned. "Why not?"

"J said Desai didn't think it would be safe for them."

She raised an eyebrow. "Not sure I like the sound of that."

"No, me neither," agreed Thaddeus. "But what else are we to do? We've tried everywhere else."

"Perhaps we should visit the nearest town with

a telegraph?" Rémy suggested. "Send one back to Desai's men in London, to ask if they can tell us anything else?"

Thaddeus shook his head. "We're a long way from anywhere big enough for that," he said, "and besides, I think they've told us everything they can. They don't know where he is any better than we do." He sighed, leaning back against the tree and shutting his double-colored eyes. "It'd be easier if I could speak some of the languages and dialects, ask people more than just what Satu had me write down. Perhaps we should have prepared better before we came on this trip."

Rémy rested a hand on his arm. "I do not think so," she said softly. "After all, we may already be too late. Delaying — that could not be a good thing."

It had now been some months since either Rémy or Thaddeus had seen their friend Maandhata Desai, who had been such an ally in their strange battle against Lord Abernathy and the war machines he had built beneath England's capital city. Desai had journeyed back to his homeland, leaving his network of operatives in London under Thaddeus's command and telling the then-policeman that he was returning to India to deal with something called the Sapphire Cutlass. None of Desai's people had been able to give

Thaddeus any more information about this curious name. Thaddeus, however, had a horrible suspicion that it was linked to the mad mechanical trail that had started in London with Abernathy and continued in France with the Comte de Cantal. While imprisoned in the Comte's monstrous volcanic dungeons, forced to listen to the man's ramblings about his power, the young man had seen for himself the peculiar tattoo that graced the Comte's chest — a short, curved sword with a glittering sapphire imbedded in the hilt: a sapphire cutlass. How could something so strange be a coincidence? Thaddeus — and Rémy too, once he had explained it all — had been worried, not just for their friend, but also for the wider implications. If the Sapphire Cutlass — whatever it was — was behind the mania of the Comte de Cantal, where else did it have influence? The Comte's insanity had resulted in the destruction of an entire mountain that took with it a whole town, but if both he and Abernathy had had their way, things would have been much, much worse. If there was a driving force behind these desires, stoking them — what was coming next?

The problem was that Desai seemed to have disappeared completely. His men had given Thaddeus as much help as they could via telegram, whizzing typed messages back and forth across the vast distances from London to cities such as Bombay, Madras, and Bangalore. They had suggested towns he might have visited, routes he might have taken, people he might have been to see, but each time the airship had arrived somewhere new, its crew full of expectation, their hopes had been dashed. No one had seen Desai or knew where he was.

Or at least, that was what they *said*.

Privately, both Rémy and Thaddeus had the sense that at least some, if not all, of the people that they had met along the way were hiding something. None of them wanted to talk about Desai or where he might be, as if they were scared of what might happen if they were overheard. As for the Sapphire Cutlass, well — mention those words and people might as well have turned to stone. Which, as far as the crew of the airship went, made the search even more important. It was unfortunate, then, that they had run out of ideas as to where to go next. India was a big, big place to search, even with the help of a device as miraculous as a ruby-powered airship.

Rémy absently opened her bag and took out her puzzle box, turning it around in her hands as she looked at the haphazard route they had followed to date. The last village they had visited, situated right on the edges of the jungle, had been so small that it had been immediately apparent that it wouldn't take them long to find out what they needed to know. The place had been made up of fewer than twenty small houses, and as far as Rémy could make out, was mostly populated by the very young and the very old. Perhaps anyone who was able to work was out in the fields, although the crops had seemed sparse and unkept as the shadow of the airship had drifted across them.

The people had been terrified of the airship, which wasn't surprising. J had landed it a little way away and the group had walked in rather than touching down directly beside the houses. Desai was not there, and according to everyone they had shown Thaddeus's written questions to — the entire village — he never had been. Polite as they all were, it had been very clear that the people had just wanted them to go.

"So, have you had any more luck with that?"

Thaddeus's question jolted Rémy out of her thoughts and she found him nodding at the puzzle box.

"No," Rémy sighed, twisting one of its small outer panels so that a hinge folded in on itself. "Every time I think I have made progress, *voila*! Another hinge appears that I cannot open without undoing what came before." She made a sound of annoyance in her throat. "Truly, I am beginning to think that the old woman was just playing with me."

Thaddeus smiled, his fingers brushing hers as he took the puzzle from her and toyed with it. They had been trying to open it ever since they had left France, tantalized by the thought that whatever was inside might help Rémy locate her fabled lost brother.

"Don't give up," he told her. "Not that I think you ever would. Rémy Brunel always sees things through to the end, no matter how difficult the journey."

Rémy looked at him. Somewhere over the course of the past few months, things had changed between them. Perhaps it was just that she no longer had her opal to tell her his every thought, although Rémy somehow felt it was more than that. Things were easier between them. They were closer — they fit together better. They understood each other, and where they didn't, they at least tried to.

Maybe this is just what it feels like when you really love someone, she thought. *Maybe this is what happens when you find the person you should m—*

"What?" Thaddeus asked her with a laugh, as she continued to gaze at him, lost in her thoughts.

Rémy shook her head, a little shocked at where her mind had been leading her.

Thaddeus reached out and stroked his fingers along her jaw. "Come here," he murmured, pulling her gently toward him.

Her lips had almost touched his when there was a loud bang. A fraction of a second later, something thudded into the tree behind them, just inches above Thaddeus's head, splinters of sharp bark exploding from the impact.

Chapter 3

THE JEWELED MAN

$\mathcal{R}$émy and Thaddeus were on their feet in a second. Even as the sound of the explosion faded in their ears, another took its place, and this time Thaddeus felt the rush of air as a bullet whistled past his cheek. From somewhere unseen, Dita began to scream. The sound echoed around the clearing, reverberating off the yellow stone walls of the ruined temple. Primed for flight, scanning the edges of the forest, he saw movement and knew that something had found them.

"Soldiers!" Rémy gasped.

Men poured out of the jungle, lithe and quick, moving toward them like shadows — they were halfway across the clearing before Thaddeus and Rémy had even had a chance to react. Thaddeus set off for the airship at a flat run, knowing that Rémy was right beside him.

Thaddeus glanced over his shoulder. The men were still coming, rushing at them like a square-jawed tide. They were all huge: bronze skin, their chins densely bearded, their shoulders broad. They wore blue and white: jewel-bright turquoise for the *pagris* wrapped around their heads and the loose trousers over their legs, purest white for the shirts that were fastened about their waists with wide gold cummerbunds. They moved in two waves: the first carrying huge, ornately curved swords, the second armed with rifles.

They were like no soldiers Thaddeus had ever seen, but that didn't make them any less terrifying.

From the corner of his eye, Thaddeus saw Rémy leap up one of the temple's crushed walls, scattering splinters of stone dust in her wake. Sunlight glinted on silver as a blade slashed after her, missing her by inches. Rémy jumped, twisting in the air as if on an imaginary trapeze, turning a somersault and then lashing out one leg to catch her attacker in the jaw before landing squarely back on two feet. Thaddeus didn't see what happened to the swordsman — he had his own worries as another of the soldiers lunged toward him, his vicious blade swinging directly for Thaddeus's head.

The Englishman threw himself forward, dropping to his knees and using the momentum to crash into his attacker's legs — nowhere near as elegant a move as Rémy's, but just as effective. Thaddeus was still no prizefighter, but he'd grown fitter during their journey in the airship. The craft was heavy and required muscle to keep her on course, muscle that he put to good use now. Their attackers were bigger than either Rémy or Thaddeus, but Thaddeus wasn't intending to fight. All they needed to do was get to the airship.

He skidded under another blade that flew toward him, leaning backward so that it passed over his chin in a curve that, had it been an inch lower, would have cut his throat. Thaddeus sprang back to his feet, glancing sideways to see where Rémy was. She'd vaulted the second wall, having leveled another swordsman. Thaddeus could see the huge man in the act of stumbling back to the ground even as Little Bird flew out of his clutches.

There came another scream from Dita.

"I will go for her," Rémy shouted as she dodged another soldier.

"No — Rémy — wait!"

Thaddeus's shout came far too late to stop her — Rémy had already dropped out of sight over the far side of the temple wall. Thaddeus had no time to worry as another two soldiers came at him. Breathing hard, lungs burning with effort, he sidestepped them by feigning a lunge to the right before dodging left. By the time they had corrected their footing he was past them and almost at the airship.

"J," he bellowed over the strange silence of the attack. "Get the airship up!"

"'Ere," said the boy, appearing on the ramp, "what's —"

"Attack," Thaddeus said through gasping breaths. "Get her up!"

J saw the soldiers, his ruddy face paling. "Where's Dita?"

"Rémy's gone to get her. J — quickly!"

J, looking stunned, threw him the small axe they used to sever the airship's guide ropes. Thaddeus ran to the first one, swinging his arm and bringing the blade down across it, not even attempting to untie the knot. It cut cleanly, flicking into the air like something alive. The airship immediately began to lift. Thaddeus ran for the next tether.

"Wait," J cried, "we got to wait for the others!"

"We will," Thaddeus shouted back, already at the second rope, arm swinging back. "We'll pick them up, but we have to —"

Just like that, the soldiers were on them. Thaddeus dodged as one of them sliced at him with his sword, the blade coming so close that he heard the whistle as it only just missed him. He fought back, swinging the axe and cracking it into his attacker's jaw, but he might as well have been fighting a forest fire with a glass of water. He stumbled backward, crashing into one of the temple's crumbling walls, the pain of connecting with hard rock jarring him badly. A second soldier came at him as the first regrouped, his face a cold mask of determination. Behind him were more men, surging closer by the second, all with their weapons drawn and ready. Thaddeus ducked another blade, swinging wildly at the airship's third guide rope. The rope came free as he parried a fresh blow and dived beneath yet another cruel blade.

The airship swung around above his head, nose still tethered to the ground but the rest of her straining toward the sky. Thaddeus had the sudden image of it leaving without them — drifting away into the sky without her crew, to sail the skies of the world alone.

But that couldn't — must not — happen. If it did, it would mean the rest of them would all be captured or, worse, killed. He narrowly avoided another attack and then lunged forward, throwing all his weight at his nearest assailant. Caught off guard for a split second, the soldier stumbled backward, his head connecting with the brightly painted Union Jack emblazoned on the underside of the airship's hull. The man's eyes rolled back and he fell to the ground, unconscious.

Thaddeus hardly had time to take a breath before he was attacked again. This time he thought he was done for, but something dropped out of the sky, yelling like a banshee. It knocked his assailant to the ground and he scrambled away. Thaddeus's savior was J, who had jumped from the airship's wildly tilting ramp onto the brute's back.

Thaddeus grabbed a handful of J's collar and dragged him away. "Get back on board!" he shouted. "I'm going to cut the last rope!"

"I ain't leaving Dita!"

"Neither am I! Rémy will get her!"

J squirmed away from him and then, before Thaddeus had a chance to stop him, started running. Thaddeus, cursing, watched J dodge one of the men and realized he was out of time. They had to keep hold of the airship, or they were done for — it was their only advantage.

He'd left the guide rope closest to the ramp until last, but still — cutting it without anyone on board was risky. With no one to control it, the airship could drift away into the endless blue Indian sky, but Thaddeus had no choice. He severed the final rope and then heaved himself up onto the flapping ramp, kicking out at another soldier on his way.

The airship leapt into the air, free of the ground at last. Thaddeus dragged the ramp up and ran to the controls, bringing the craft around hard a-port to stop her nose from smashing against the temple walls. For just a second, Thaddeus found himself face-to-face with a many-armed diva as she smiled at him from the stone archway into which she'd been carved hundreds of years before. Then the airship turned, tipping away from the temple and toward the jungle.

Below them the men were watching, evidently awed by the sight of such a flying machine. Thaddeus ignored them, searching for signs of Rémy, Dita, and J. With any luck, he could whisk all of them from the ground — the guide ropes were still hanging below the ship, which was as close as he could get to a ladder at this moment.

Then he caught sight of Dita and J, and Thaddeus's heart sank. The two children had both been caught. They struggled in the clutches of their captors, but it was clear that neither of them would get away that easily. Of Rémy, though, there was no sign.

There was more movement at the edge of the clearing. The foliage moved, rippling as if disturbed by a breeze. Then it parted, and someone new emerged. Another man, who sat astride a grand white horse, which was dressed even more spectacularly than the soldiers. Jewels of every hue glinted in the creature's braided mane and along the leather of its harness. Its rider, though, outdid them all. He too was in silk of blue and gold, but the very fabric of his garments seemed to be spun through with diamonds so that he shone like a cut gem. His head was wrapped and adorned in a sumptuous array of jewels that glinted in the afternoon sun.

This man held his chin high, looking straight at Thaddeus through the window of the airship. He rode to meet it, urging his horse forward as if facing off with an enemy in battle, and the animal was so used to his command that he only required one hand on the reigns. With the other, he gestured to the two men holding Dita and J without even turning to look.

The children were wrestled forward, still squirming, until they stood beside the horse. Then they were forced to their knees.

Thaddeus's blood ran cold as he saw the men's swords leveled at the throats of his two young friends.

"You will listen to me, commander of this ship of the air," came the man's faint voice, filtering through to Thaddeus, safe in the airship above. "You will follow me and my men, and you will surrender it to us. If you do not, the lives of your two companions here will be forfeit. Understand that I will cut their throats without hesitation should you fail to comply."

Without waiting for a reply, the man on horseback waved his arm again. Instantly, the soldiers formed up in a column of three lines. One more signed command from their leader and they all set off, the rider leading them into the jungle, dragging Dita and J along with them.

Thaddeus had no choice.

The airship followed.

Chapter 4

A JUNGLE PALACE

The soldiers marched for hours, until the slivered moon was high in the sky and Rémy could barely see through the shadows that surrounded her. She kept her eyes on the airship, flying low above the tree line, blocking out a trail of stars as it went. She was beginning to wonder whether the jeweled man and his troops were planning to march all the way to Pondicherry when a shout echoed through the foliage — a sharp order sent back from the front.

Rémy realized with a start that they had obviously reached their destination. She'd been so focused on keeping track of the airship and not making a sound over the uneven ground that she'd missed what was ahead of them. There, reaching above the dark mass of jungle, she could see walls looming into the sky, a luminous mass of white in the moonlight. They rose high above the forest — higher even, Rémy thought, than where the highest seat in the Cirque de la Lune's Big Top had been, though not as high as her trapeze had flown on those nights that she had performed in front of the crowds. The wall stretched for a long way in either direction. In the center and on the ends of the wall were built large, square towers with domed roofs that were shining softly in the moonlight as if they were coated with silver. Beneath the domes, standing stiffly alert at their posts as they looked out over the forest, were soldiers armed with rifles.

Another shout, and the column halted so swiftly that Rémy almost walked into the back of the two men making up the rear. She darted behind the nearest tree, peering out as a loud creaking sound echoed into the night. Beneath the sentry post in the center of the wall, illuminated in the yellow glow from two huge torches pinioned either side of them, were two massive doors. Rémy watched as they slowly opened, and even from where she hid, she could see the glint of the metal spikes that studded the carved dark wood. There came another shout and the soldiers, led by the jeweled man on his magnificent horse, marched forward beneath the arch.

The airship lifted over the wall, and then dropped out of sight. The doors creaked again as they closed behind the last of the troops, shutting Rémy out — although not before she caught a glimpse of the airship, touching down amid the torrent of soldiers.

Careful to avoid drawing the gaze of the sentries, Rémy slipped closer. The jungle pressed right up against the walls, which seemed strange to her. Surely the best way of keeping such a place secure was to make sure that no one could approach without being seen, but as it was, Rémy made it all the way to one cold, white wall. When she reached it, however, she realized that the walls were not as featureless as she had at first thought. They were peppered with holes and cracks of varying sizes; the fractures pockmarked the surface of the wall with what looked like delicate lace in the moonlight, but that in daylight probably displayed themselves more like a series of ugly scars. They were the signs of fierce battle — each hole had been made by a weapon — by rifles, and in some cases, small canons.

This place was old and crumbling. The troops that had attacked the airship's crew — whoever they were — were defending a relic that looked as if it should have been abandoned years ago. *Still,* Rémy thought, standing at the base of the wall and looking up it, *good for me . . .* She checked the sentries in their posts. They were still staring out over the forest, and the light cast by the torches at the gate did not reach far enough to touch her shadowed spot. Rémy took a breath and began to climb. Within minutes, the handholds provided by the wall's battle scars had helped her reach the top. Rémy crouched there, barely even out of breath, her black clothes as dark as the shadows around her, and looked down into a well of golden light.

She'd expected a fort of some kind — an ugly, bare patch of earth crammed with low barrack buildings for the soldiers. But what Rémy saw was anything but ugly, even though it was as crumbling and ancient as the walls on which she now crouched. Within stood a palace of white stone, gleaming in the moonlight like one of the gems on its owner's hand. Yes, some of the columns were crumbling with age, and there were signs of rifle strikes among the ornate carvings that decked its windows and its many roofs. Its domes — far larger than the ones over the clueless sentries' heads — were dull gray instead of silver, but its beauty still took Rémy's breath away. She wondered how many rooms there were within its inner walls. From here she couldn't even count the windows, and there were at least four floors. It was magnificent, despite or perhaps even because of its age.

A sound drew her attention back to the vast courtyard in front of the palace's steps. The airship had landed in the center, next to a carved stone fountain that must have run dry years before. Thaddeus was being dragged from the airship. He stumbled under his captors' grip and was pushed to his knees, lined up in the dust beside Dita and J. Wordlessly, a soldier stepped toward each of them, drawing their curved swords and holding them at their necks. Anger swelled in Rémy's heart as she saw Dita flinch and tremble as the cold metal touched her skin.

The jeweled man had slipped from his saddle, handing the reins of his horse to a servant who bowed deeply before leading the creature away. The man then circled the airship thoughtfully, disappearing from her view as he walked around the front and then reappeared at the propeller end. She saw that he had something in his hand — he was throwing it from one and catching it in the other as he walked, and it glinted with the reflection of the flickering light from the torches on the walls. Rémy almost gasped as she realized what it was. Her puzzle box!

There was a brief commotion as a new man entered the scene, descending the steps of the palace at a slow, dignified pace. Dressed in pure white, this man was older, with wisps of gray-white hair escaping the *pagri* wrapped around his head. He held himself regally, and as Rémy watched, she saw a ripple move through the assembled troops as he passed by — a straightening of the shoulders, a lifting of the chins. Clearly this man, too, held great power here, despite his lack of ostentatious jewelry. He stood before the airship's nose, his hands clasped behind his back. He did not seem in the least impressed, but instead regarded the craft with something like contempt.

The jeweled man completed his circuit of the ship and moved to stand with the man in white. They conferred quietly for a few moments, apparently disagreeing about something, though only mildly. The older man eventually brought his hands in front of him, spreading his palms in a gesture somewhat like a shrug.

The jeweled man nodded once, and then turned to the silent soldiers still standing at attention in the rows they had formed after entering the palace gates.

"This," he began, his deep voice echoing around the courtyard, "is a historic day, my friends. This — this!"

He waved at the airship. "This magnificent ship of the air will change our fortunes and the fortunes of this great country forever. For too many years we have toiled without hope, dreaming of freeing all of India from the foul grip of colonization. Now, here, with the help of this marvelous contraption and the others like it that we shall build together — we will at last achieve our goals. Together, we will smite the British and their armies who ransack our land! We will take back our food, we will take back our cities and towns and villages! We will take back our sovereignty!"

A cheer rumbled up through the flickering torchlight, rolling over Rémy like a wave of thunder. The soldiers below all drew their curved swords, shouting and waving their weapons in the air until the glow of the glinting fire reflected in the blades was a blinding mass of light.

The man in white, Rémy noted, did not cheer. He stared straight ahead, his face impassive apart from, she thought, the slightest flicker of something that could have been fury. Although it was gone before it had ever really been there at all.

The jeweled man raised his hands for silence, and it fell as quickly as it had in the jungle when the tiger had stalked the chital. Rémy dared not move a muscle, perched as she was atop the wall. If any of them were to see her, there were a thousand ways for her to die at the hands of these men.

"Go now, to your duties," the jeweled man ordered. "I must rest, for tomorrow is a new day, and it will dawn on a new era for us all."

The troops, as one, bowed low to their leader. They moved off, some taking up posts around the great courtyard, others disappearing through a large arch on the far side of the palace that Rémy couldn't see into but assumed was a barracks. Others still entered a smaller arch that framed a slope that led beneath the palace.

Rémy watched as Thaddeus, Dita, and J were pulled roughly to their feet. Thaddeus tried to say something, but one of the soldiers clubbed him roughly about the face with enough force that Rémy winced, feeling a fresh surge of fury burst through her. Thaddeus, stunned, did not try to speak again, and a moment later the jeweled man waved a peremptory hand. The three prisoners were dragged in the direction of the small archway that led into the palace foundations. She watched as they disappeared through it and out of her sight.

The courtyard was almost empty. Besides the four

guards who circled the airship, just the jeweled man and the man in white remained. The jeweled man looked proudly at his new acquisition before tossing Rémy's puzzle box into the air once more. He made a remark that made the man in white bow his head, as if in obeisance. Then he strode toward the palace steps, taking them two at a time and swishing through a door that opened for him as if by magic. After another moment of silent contemplation, the man in white turned and followed.

{Chapter 5}

BREAKING IN

$\mathscr{S}$till crouched in the shadows atop the wall, Rémy looked down on the empty scene below her. Even with four guards, she could probably retake the airship alone, but doing that would no doubt condemn her friends to death before she'd have a chance to ransom it for their return. She imagined them now, being shoved roughly into a dingy cell in the lowest part of the palace. No, she had to free them first. Which meant getting in unseen. Now that most of the soldiers had left the courtyard, taking their torches with them, the light inside the walls was far dimmer. There were still lights burning, though — two torches on each wall, like the ones beside the great wooden door in the outer wall. For Rémy not to attract the attention of either the guards on the wall or the four standing at attention around the airship, she needed a diversion.

Lying flat on top of the wide wall, Rémy slowly pried out a piece of the crumbling stonework. At first she didn't think it was going to budge — the wall was sturdier than it looked — but her nimble fingers finally managed to pull free a chunk the size of her puzzle box. Puffs of chalky dust floated away into the hot night air as she lifted it carefully onto the wall before sitting up. She chose a spot in the forest — close enough to the wall to be of concern to the sentries but far enough away not to be easily inspected from their posts — then drew back her arm and threw.

The piece of stone was swallowed by the night almost immediately, arcing in a smooth but invisible curve from Rémy's hand into the jungle outside the palace walls. By sheer luck she must have chosen the sleeping place of a family of monkeys, because there came a sudden and terrible cacophony of shrieks, followed by the shaking of not just leaves, but the entire tree.

As she'd hoped, both sentries on that side of the palace were suddenly instantly awake, fervently searching the forest for a sign of something coming toward them. They were so intent on what was happening below them that they didn't see her slip from her perch on the wall and descend into the shadows of the courtyard. Once back on the ground, Rémy moved quickly, keeping to the edges, as far away from the sentries on duty at the airship as possible. She made for the archway she'd seen Thaddeus, Dita, and J being dragged toward: the smaller one that led below the palace.

To get to it Rémy had to pass directly in front of the palace steps. She darted from one pool of shadows to another, stopping every few minutes to make sure she had made no noise. The courtyard seemed even bigger now that she was down on the ground — the fountain she had dismissed as old and disused was, she realized now, almost as big as the airship itself. The flagstones beneath her feet were carved from large slabs of marble, white and veined with lines of mineral that glimmered slightly even in the darkness. The palace itself was built of the same marble, carved and curved and in daylight, Rémy thought it quite likely, beautiful despite its age.

She reached the archway — which would be large enough to take a cart and oxen without its driver having to leave his seat — and slipped inside. The ground sloped down and away. Rémy descended the path, a solid iron gate blocking her way just a few feet inside. Beyond it, lights burned almost as brightly as if it were day, and Rémy quickly flattened herself against the wall as she realized there was movement there, too. Soldiers and servants bustled about beyond the barrier, moving barrels and sacks of food from one place to another — besides wherever her friends were being kept, this level was obviously storage for the rest of the palace, too. There was too much activity beyond the gate for her to pick its lock without being seen.

Cursing silently, Rémy looked around. A flight of stone steps curved upward and out of sight to her left. Since she seemed to have no other option, she dodged over and ascended them quickly — if anyone happened to be coming the other way, she'd be caught for sure, for the torch burning on the wall meant here there were no shadows big enough to melt into. Rémy sighed in relief as she made it to the next floor. The stairway opened out into a wide corridor, which led to many small rooms and antechambers. It was cooler here, she noted — the marble of the palace walls helping to quell the incessant heat, at least a little.

Rémy headed along the corridor, hoping to find another way down into the lower levels. This floor seemed to be the servants' quarters. The few open doors showed her sparse, basic living arrangements of low beds and plain, dusty floors. Another room had rows of tables lined up almost like a schoolroom, except that each surface was piled with rich fabrics: silks and brocades, poplins and charmeuse. Rémy could imagine the room flooded with sunny daylight, filled with activity as the men and women who worked there sewed the jeweled man yet another extraordinarily beautiful outfit. For a split second she wondered whether any of the jewels they used to adorn his clothes would be kept in there, too, but despite the temptation to look, she forced herself not to investigate. Rémy Brunel was a thief no longer, but sometimes . . . just sometimes . . .

With a silent sigh, she moved onward, past door after closed door. A sound echoed ahead of her — footsteps, coming closer. Panicked, Rémy looked around, but there was nothing in the corridor to hide behind. She tried one door, turning the circular handle silently, but it appeared to be locked. Moving to another as the footfalls grew ever louder, she found that to be locked, too. She glanced over her shoulder, wondering if she could make it back to the flight of stairs, but realized that would be the height of folly — there was more light there, more chance that she'd be trapped between someone coming up and whoever this was, coming down.

Darting to the other side of the corridor, she tried another handle. This time the door gave and she slipped inside, finding herself in darkness. She leaned against the door, leveling her breathing, as the person outside passed, footsteps echoing into the distance without pause. Rémy sighed in relief.

"Who's there?"

The voice made her jump. Rémy's instinct was to drop to a crouch, and she did, staying near the door and hoping that the darkness was enough to conceal her. Rémy slowed her breathing — a circus trick she'd been taught long ago to help her calm herself on the wire — and prayed that whomever she'd stirred from slumber would drop off again just as quickly.

It seemed, however, that Rémy's luck was running low.

"I know you are there," said a man's voice, deep and low, melodic. "By the door. Show yourself, please."

Still Rémy said nothing. A strange sound echoed from the direction of the voice — a clank, followed by a rattle and the sound of something dragging itself through the darkness. Then the sound of a match being struck sent Rémy's heart plummeting. A pale, flickering light bloomed into the room as the owner of the voice lit a candle.

Rémy stood, swiftly, her hand already back on the door handle, ready to run. The figure on the bed was still moving, legs swinging over its low edge as the man's feet reached the stone floor.

"Wait," said the figure, "don't go . . ."

Something about the voice and the figure made Rémy hesitate, just for a second. She turned to look at the man, taking in the long, unkempt hair and beard.

She gasped.

"Desai!"

{Chapter 6}

BREAKING OUT

$\mathcal{D}$esai, who was in the process of trying to stand up, looked up at her with sharply narrowed eyes that suddenly widened in recognition.

"Rémy Brunel! What in the name of Shiva are you doing here?"

Rémy was across the room in a second, standing angrily before her old friend as he got slowly to his feet.

"We came to look for you," she hissed furiously, "but we were attacked by the soldiers of this palace and the jeweled man who commands them. They have taken Thaddeus, J, and Dita — they are here, somewhere below our feet even now. And now I find that you, our friend, the man we came to find, are in league with the monster who took them and stole the airship!"

Desai blinked at her with hooded lids. "Believe me, Miss Brunel, at this moment I am as much a prisoner as they." He raised his right arm, and the clanking sound Rémy had heard minutes earlier came again.

It was only then that Rémy saw the chain. It was thick and heavy, attached to a cuff that circled Desai's arm — an arm that, she saw, was far thinner than the last time she had seen him. The other end of the chain was fastened to a ring set fast into the stone floor.

Rémy glanced around the room. It was as bare as the others she had seen, with the exception of a small table standing close to the bed, on which was a pile of paper and an ink pen standing upright in its well. Desai's chain was just long enough to allow him to move between the bed and the table, but no farther.

"What is happening here?" Rémy asked.

Desai gave her a faint smile. His hair had grayed even more since their last meeting. "The 'Jeweled Man,' as you call him, is the raja of this palace and he wants what I have up here," he tapped his forehead with one thin finger. "Or rather, his right-hand man, Sahoj, does. They intend to keep me here until I give it to them."

Rémy fumbled beneath her shirt. She'd foregone her customary corset since reaching India — in the heat it was just unbearable — but wore her usual black shirt and the belt in which she still carried the tools of her former trade. She pulled out her pack of lock-picking tools, folded neatly in the small leather case that Gustave had given her a lifetime ago.

"Sit," she ordered, indicating the bed, and then as Desai did so, she knelt before him and took his right hand. The skin around the cuff was raw, and she tried not to agitate it further as she worked on the lock.

"Tell me more about the jeweled man," she whispered as she worked.

She glanced up to see Desai looking away into the shadows, a thoughtful frown on his face. Then he looked at her with a slight smile, as if to dispel what had caused the frown. "It will take a long time to explain. Perhaps it should wait . . ."

"Until we have escaped this place? *Mais oui.* Later, then . . . *voila!*" she whispered triumphantly as the cuff slid undone under her fingers. "You are free, my friend. Now, let us see about the others, yes?"

Desai stood, rubbing his wrist. "There is another way down to the cells. We will need to go through the kitchens — they have their own access, so that the cooks may easily deliver food to the guards for the prisoners."

Rémy frowned. "There are still many people up and about. You are sure we will not be seen?"

"Oh, I am absolutely sure we will be seen," Desai said grimly, "but I have known this place for a long, long time. There are people who will be willing to help. But Rémy — getting to our friends, getting them out of their prisons, even, that is one thing. But getting out of the palace? That is quite another. As soon as the alarm has sounded, we will be trapped. And you may be able to scale the walls, my dear, but I guarantee you that such a feat is beyond me."

"Ah — but that is why we will retake the airship," said Rémy. "In the air we will outrun them without any trouble."

Desai frowned again. "Airship. You used that word before. I have not heard of such a thing. What is it?"

Rémy grinned. "You will see. Another of the Professor's inventions, Desai, and one that meant we could follow you here, to this place. Now, are you ready? We are wasting time with all this chat!"

Desai turned and grabbed a sheet from the bed, holding it out to her. "Wrap this around yourself. Cover your head, also. My face is known here and prisoner or not I am not much to remark upon. But yours is not and will not go unnoticed." He nodded as Rémy did as she was told. "Good. Now, follow closely and be alert."

Once out of the room, Desai walked quickly to the end of the corridor, and Rémy stayed as close to him as she could. They saw no one as they turned the corner and entered another corridor, this time where the doors were more widely spaced. Ahead, noise floated to them along with a glow that partially dispelled the nighttime gloom. There came the rattle of what sounded like pots and pans, and the occasional shout of an order or the hiss of steam rising.

Rémy pulled her makeshift cloak more closely around her face as they entered the kitchens. There were people everywhere, working diligently as they chopped vegetables or stirred huge pots of richly scented sauces. Rémy's heart pounded, expecting one of the cooks to see them at any moment and raise the alarm. But when one man did look up and see

Desai, his eyes merely widened for a moment before he bowed his head in what seemed to be a mark of respect.

Desai took no notice, hurrying through the kitchen, passing bench after bench of foods being prepared and spices being crushed. Despite their situation, Rémy's stomach rumbled — the brace of rabbits she'd caught earlier in the day had remained uncooked, and she was very hungry. She thought about slipping out a hand to snag a carrot as she passed, but thought better of it.

Her companion came to an abrupt stop as another cook stepped out in front of him. At first Rémy thought that Desai was about to be challenged, but instead the man offered the same nod of respect the first had given. This time Desai responded in kind — they obviously knew each other. Desai leaned forward and spoke rapidly into the man's ear. The cook's gaze flicked to Rémy's for a second and then back to Desai before nodding quickly and turning. Desai looked over his shoulder at Rémy. Evidently they were to follow.

The cook led them to another circular flight of stairs, also lit with a burning torch. They descended quickly and found themselves on the lower level, though this area was far darker than the one Rémy had failed to gain access to earlier. Passageways led in two directions, left and right, and both were lined with the sturdy doors of many cells. Silently, the cook pointed left. Desai clasped his arm firmly in thanks, and without another word the man had gone, vanishing back up the steps to resume his work.

Desai and Rémy moved quickly along the passageway. Rémy glanced in through each of the barred doors as they went, searching for Thaddeus, Dita, and J. Some of the cells were empty, but others held pitiful-looking prisoners, thin men with protruding ribs and long, straggly hair, who all seemed as if they had been there for a long, long time. Desai glanced left and right, seeing but passing on just as quickly.

They found their friends in neighboring cells: the soldiers had separated Dita from Thaddeus and J and imprisoned her beside them. J and Dita were kneeling on the filthy floor, grasping each other's hands through the bars. Rémy, still concealed by her "cloak," felt her heart leap in relief at the sight of Thaddeus with his back against the cell wall, his forearms resting on his drawn-up knees.

Thaddeus barely showed any interest as Desai and Rémy appeared in front of him. He merely glanced up at Desai before dropping his gaze briefly to Rémy and then looking away again. A second later, though, his double-colored eyes flashed wide with recognition and he scrambled to his feet.

"My god! *Desai!* What are you —? How —?"

"No time, my friend, no time. Rémy, quickly, can you free this lock?"

"Rémy!" Thaddeus exclaimed again as she threw off the sheet and stepped forward, once more reaching for her lock picks.

Rémy smiled at him through the bars. "You didn't think I'd leave you behind, did you? Where you go, I go. Don't you know that by now?"

Thaddeus smiled back, fixing her with a look of such intensity that she found her heart leaping again, though for an entirely different reason.

"Can't you get Dita out first?" J pleaded as she turned her attention to the lock. "I 'ate 'er bein' in there alone."

"Better for us to get out first, J," Thaddeus said softly, moving to the bars and looking down the passageway. "That way if there's trouble, you and I can deal with it while Rémy frees Dita."

Rémy caught J's nod of agreement in the corner of her eye as she worked. These locks were more difficult than the one on Desai's cuff. She cursed under her breath as the barrel refused to turn.

"How long?" Desai asked, his quiet voice strained as he, too, kept an eye out.

"I will be as quick as I can," Rémy murmured calmly, keeping her concentration entirely on the lock.

"I'll be back," said Desai. "Be quick, Rémy. You must be the swiftest you have ever been, my dear."

He vanished up the passageway. Rémy half expected to hear the sounds of fighting echo out of the darkness that flowed into his wake, but there was nothing but silence. Still she worked, rotating the barrel again and again, until, at last —

Click.

She heaved a sigh of relief. The door opened, creaking on its rusted hinges so loudly in the quiet that she winced. Thaddeus grabbed the bars to hold it still, waving J out ahead of him as Rémy swiftly moved to the lock on Dita's cell. The little girl wrapped her hands around the bars, eyes wide as she watched Rémy's nimble fingers get to work.

Desai returned a few minutes later. "If we are quick now, we will have a clear route to the outer courtyard," he told them. "But we must be fast."

"I have to find the jeweled man — the raja you spoke of," Rémy said, her eyes fixed on the second lock.

"What do you mean?" Desai asked, appalled. "We have to leave, Rémy. We are vastly outnumbered, and —"

"He has my puzzle box," she told him, still concentrating, twisting the barrel, testing the lock. "I can't leave without it. I must get it back."

Desai made a sound in his throat. "Whatever he has taken from you, Rémy, I guarantee it is not worth the risk."

"It is to me," Rémy said. "I must have it back, Desai. I *must*. You take the others and go — get the airship. You said yourself, I can scale these walls. I'll follow once I have it."

"You must be joking," said Thaddeus. "Rémy, that's crazy. They weren't looking for you before, but once the alarm is raised . . ."

"I will not leave without it, Thaddeus," said Rémy, "I will not. Understand?"

"Then I will stay, too."

"No," she told him, "I will be faster — safer — on my own."

"You will be the death of me, Rémy Brunel," Desai muttered.

"Is that so?" she answered tartly. "And here I was thinking I had freed you once already tonight."

Desai sighed. "All right. Give me a moment. But we are running out of time!"

He vanished again, moving up the passageway and back toward the stairs that led to the kitchens.

"D'acccord, d'accord," muttered Rémy, still working on the lock. It clicked suddenly, the door springing open more quietly than the first one. Dita slipped out, and J instantly clasped her in a brief, powerful hug.

Thaddeus was at Rémy's side as she straightened. He took one of her hands and squeezed it. "Please don't do this," he said softly. "Let it go, Rémy — let the puzzle box go. Only this morning you were saying you thought it was all a trick."

Rémy gave him a faint smile and squeezed his hand back again. "But what if it is *not* a trick? What if it really can tell me where my brother is?"

Thaddeus opened his mouth to reply but by then Desai was coming back along the passageway. He wasn't alone — with him was the cook Rémy had encountered earlier. He was carrying a silver tray bearing small bowls of food that smelled delicious enough to have Rémy's stomach rumbling, despite their plight.

"Go with Arund," Desai told her, picking up the sheet and thrusting it toward her. "He will help you.

Now, the rest of us must go, or we will all be caught again."

Rémy squeezed Thaddeus's hand once more, and then let go. Seconds later, she was following the man she now knew as Arund. Rémy thought he was taking her back to the kitchen stairs, but instead they hurried past them, down another darkened passageway to a different set of steps entirely. Arund didn't pause as he led her up them. These went higher than the first two flights she had encountered, and when they emerged, it was on a very different type of floor. Where the servants' level had been dusty stone, this was a sparkling-clean mosaic of black and white marble tiles, spread with intricately woven carpets. The walls were adorned with colorful tapestries and paintings, and unlike the empty corridors directly below, ornate furniture stood here and there against the walls: wooden cabinets carved with intricate scenes of the jungle, backless chairs draped with more of the rich fabrics Rémy had seen in the tailors' room on the floor below.

Arund moved quickly and silently with Rémy close in his wake, her cloak wafting in the breeze they created through the otherwise still and silent halls. Then, suddenly he stopped and turned, picking up the silver jug from his platter and holding it out to her. Rémy hesitated for a second, confused, and then took it, careful not to spill any of the water contained within while still holding her cloak closed. They moved off again, turning a corner, and as she glanced up, Rémy saw a large door at the far end of the corridor, its hammered gold gleaming in the fiery lamplight, flanked by two guards.

At first Rémy thought the platter and jug were for the inhabitant of the room behind the door, but instead Arund greeted the two soldiers and held up the silver tray. It only took a brief glance for her to see the grins on the men's faces. Arund drew them away from the door until he could place the platter on an ornate table a few feet away. He beckoned to Rémy, taking the water jug from her when she moved closer and then waving her back.

Stepping away, Rémy found the guard's shoulders turned away from her, intent on their welcome midshift snack instead of on their posts. She knew it was the only opportunity she was going to get. Arund ignored her, laughing and joking in whispers with the guards as she moved silently backward until her back was against the door.

And then, in another moment, she was through it.

The room inside was dark, no light visible apart from the pale wash of moonlight through the large window at the far end of the room. Even so, Rémy could make out the shape of a huge bed at the center of the space, its canopy hung with heavy, opulent cloth. Rémy crept closer, her eyes adjusting to the renewed dark. The room was airy, far bigger even than the kitchen she had seen downstairs. Compared to the servants' quarters, this was a different world, a world full of beautiful wonders, the colors of which she could only imagine in the gray-toned hue of night.

Rémy crept toward the bed and the tangled mass of sheets that lay at its center. As she moved closer, she saw that it was indeed the jeweled man — seeming, as such men so often did, far smaller and less significant in sleep than in life. But he wasn't what she was interested in. All Rémy wanted was her puzzle box.

Beside the bed stood a table, cluttered with trinkets that gleamed even in the faint light. And there, discarded like a toy, was her puzzle box. She picked it up, careful not to dislodge any of the other items on the tabletop, moving slowly and silently as her fingers gripped its whorled surface.

A sound echoed through the window — it was just one shout at first, but then it was a violent tide

of noise: yells, screams, the echo of rifleshot cracking against stone, the sound of booted running feet
pounding against the dirt.

The jeweled man's eyes flashed open, and they
looked straight at Rémy.

Chapter 7

ESCAPE BY AIR

Thaddeus couldn't fathom how, but the gate they had been led through when they had entered the cells was open. Not only that, the passageway that led to it from the palace's lowest level was empty. Thaddeus looked around, wondering if he was mistaken and they were actually leaving by a different route, but Desai clamped a hand to his shoulder, urging him onward.

"Hurry, we have lost much time already," his friend muttered.

"But how —?" Thaddeus began, only to be cut off by a shake of Desai's grizzled head.

"I will explain later. For now, we must take full

advantage of the lull. It will be only minutes before our time is up."

"There's four guards on the airship," J pointed out as they approached the gate. "What do we do about 'em? We ain't armed."

"All we have is the element of surprise," said Desai, adding, "Four of us, four of them. We take one each and do our best — this is our only hope."

"'Ang about," J protested. "You can't make Dita fight! She's half the size of any of 'em!"

Dita slapped J's arm, hard enough for the sound to ricochet off the stone walls around them. "Speak for yourself, dirty boy," she said in a loud whisper. "I will take mine down quicker than you will yours!"

"Pfft," J spat back, "I'd like to see you —"

Thaddeus, already through the gate, turned on the two bickering youngsters. "Now is not the time!"

"Thaddeus is right," said Desai. "Do what you can, all of you — and do it . . . now!"

They burst from the archway, crossing the court-yard at a flat run. The moonlight bounced off the white flagstones beneath their feet, sending shimmering bursts of shadow undulating across the marble as their running bodies blocked its shine. Desai was ahead, moving far faster than Thaddeus would have thought possible. They were lucky that the guards were positioned in such a way that only two were facing their position. Desai was on the first before he could even level his rifle, and Thaddeus was close behind with the second. Their cries echoed across the courtyard, bringing the other two swinging around the airship, lifting their loaded guns as the sentries on the four corners of the palace walls turned to see what the commotion was about.

Thaddeus wasn't much of a fighter — he'd always avoided the brawls his fellow street children had reveled in when growing up — but there had been plenty of times he'd needed to be handy in a scuffle as a copper on the streets of London. The guard moved to discharge his rifle, but the weapon was too cumbersome to be useful in a close-quarters fight. Thaddeus swung his left arm in an arc that knocked the weapon far enough away that the shot, when let loose, flew wide, striking one of the outer walls in a shower of glinting marble dust. Before the soldier could regain his balance, Thaddeus had punched him hard in the lower gut, finishing with a hard jab of his locked elbow to the man's chin. He went down and Thaddeus grabbed the gun as another shot echoed out of the dark. The sentries on the wall had seen what was happening and were responding accordingly, shooting down at them from above. Thaddeus swung around, trying to reload the rifle. He saw that Desai had dropped his guard, too.

Together they ducked around the airship as more rifle bullets tore up the stone around their feet. Dita and J were struggling with their guards — Thaddeus felled J's with a blow to his solar plexus as the boy struggled to swing the rifle away from the airship. Dita writhed in the grip of the last man as he lifted her clear off the ground, her legs kicking out but too short to do enough damage. J dragged the gun around and slammed its butt into the final guard's knee. The man yelled in pain and dropped Dita. J lost no time in whacking him over the head and he slumped to the ground, out cold.

"Get her up, J!" Thaddeus rasped, struggling for breath.

J ran for the airship's ramp, pulling it down and scrambling inside just as more noise began to echo across the open courtyard. Desai fired another rifle bullet in the direction of one of the sentry posts and began to reload as Thaddeus turned to see more soldiers pouring out of the barracks toward them.

He hefted his rifle up and fired above their heads. The soldiers ducked for a second and then kept coming, wielding swords rather than guns. Thaddeus felt a movement and looked down to see Dita beside him holding another rifle, a look of grim determination on her face as she sent a bullet into the surge of men coming at them.

"Desai, there are too many!" Thaddeus yelled. "Dita, get inside . . ."

A rifle bullet whistled past his head from the wall again, narrowly missing Thaddeus and smacking into the wooden body of the airship. Thaddeus glanced at the damage — minimal, thank god — and then heard a hissing sound above him. He looked up to see the balloon filling, replacing the gas he'd released to land a few hours earlier. His heart pounded in relief as the craft, buoyancy restored, began to lift off.

Thaddeus, Desai, and Dita leapt for the ramp, rushing up it and into the ship as she lifted away from the cold white marble. Within seconds they were rising out of reach of the soldiers on the ground, although rifle bullets still thudded against the airship's wooden hull.

"One of those bullets hits the balloon and we're all

done for!" J yelled, sitting at the airship's controls as he brought her about. "She'll go up like a firecracker!"

As if someone outside had heard him, a rough yell echoed from the palace. Thaddeus, in the process of pulling the ramp up, paused and saw through the chink still left open, the jeweled man leaning out of a high window just above them, screaming at his men below.

"Do not harm the ship of the sky," he was shouting. "Death to any of you who damage her beyond repair!"

Thaddeus's blood ran cold, not at the man's commanding voice, but at the sight of who else stood at the window with him. It was Rémy, her throat caught beneath his crushing fingers. She was gasping for breath, struggling against his grip but obviously losing the fight.

"J," he shouted to the front of the cabin, "hold the ship still!"

"What?" J shouted back. "Are you mad?"

Thaddeus dropped the ramp. It fell back on its hinges, jerking the airship sharply to one side. The airship was still rising, the end of the open ramp just feet from the palace walls, almost close enough for anyone to reach out and grab them, but not quite. Thaddeus could see soldiers crowding against the lower windows, aiming to do just that — leaning out as far as they could but still unable to touch their fingertips to the escaping craft.

They were almost level with the jeweled man's window, his long fingers still digging into the moon-pale skin of Rémy's neck. Her struggles were becoming weaker, her knees buckling.

"Put her down," ordered the man, his eyes glinting cruelly in the moonlight. "Put the ship of the air back down, or I will squeeze every last breath out of this whelp before you can turn away."

At that, Rémy forced herself around to face Thaddeus, her eyes defiant though she could clearly hardly breathe. She moved one arm and something sailed toward Thaddeus, dropping with a thump onto the airship's wooden floor.

Her puzzle box.

Thaddeus leveled the rifle in his hands at the jeweled man's head. "Let her go," he said, more calmly than he felt, "or I will take your head off, here and now."

The man grinned, showing his teeth in a show of hateful, swaggering arrogance. "You would not dare. You might hit her. Desperation, my friend. It is a sign that you have already lost."

Thaddeus moved the rifle just a fraction to the right and fired. There was an almighty sound as the bullet ripped into the stone window frame beside the jeweled man's head, shattering a hole in the white marble and filling the air with shards as sharp as razors. The jeweled man screamed and raised his arms to shield his face, letting Rémy go in the process. She sagged against the window, gasping for breath.

"Jump!" Thaddeus shouted at her, the airship still rising. "Rémy, for pity's sake, jump!"

Rémy, still gasping, threw her legs over the window frame and leapt wildly at the ramp, which was now almost above her head. Her fingers slipped, grasping at the wood, searching for but not finding purchase. Thaddeus dropped the rifle and lunged for her, throwing himself down stomach-first on the ramp and grabbing at her wrists.

The airship rose into the air, over the roof of the palace and away. As Thaddeus dragged Rémy to safety, the last thing they heard was the jeweled man.

"Follow them!" he screamed, leaning out of his window, his face bleeding where the splinters of his fine marble palace had struck him with a thousand tiny pinpricks. "Don't let them get away! Follow them! On pain of your deaths, *follow them!*"

"Are you all right?" Thaddeus sat on the floor beside Rémy, stroking her hair out of her face. "Rémy?"

She looked up at him, nodding faintly, still trying to catch her breath. There were red marks on her throat where the jeweled man's fingers had tried to choke the life from her body. *"D'accord,"* she whispered hoarsely, *"d'accord."*

He pulled her toward him, wrapping his arms around her and holding her against his chest. "You have got to stop trying to get yourself killed," he told her, and had the vague idea that it wasn't the first time he'd told her such a thing.

He heard her laugh, her breath on his skin warm through his shirt. "You worry too much. Anyway, you say that as if it is always my fault."

He sighed and pulled back. "Well, that time was, wasn't it?"

Rémy shrugged and looked around for the puzzle box, still lying on the floor of the airship. "I had to get it back, Thaddeus. I had to."

She got to her feet and he followed. The airship bumped a little in a sudden breeze, and Thaddeus saw Desai grip the back of J's chair as he stared at the controls in wonder.

"This is — this is remarkable," Desai was muttering. "I have never experienced anything like it."

"She's a beauty, ain't she?" J said proudly, rubbing the airship's control panel with affection.

"It is a wonder," agreed Desai, and then looked a little wobbly as another puff of wind bumped against the airship. "Oh dear. I think perhaps this mode of travel takes some getting used to . . ."

"Don't worry," Dita assured him airily, "you will soon get your air legs, Mister."

Desai looked at her curiously and then held out one hand. "I do not believe we have met, Miss . . ."

"Dita," Dita told him, shaking his hand. "I am pleased to know you, sir."

Desai smiled. "And I you, Dita. Rarely have I seen someone so small acquit herself with such aplomb," he told her, and the little girl glowed in the light of such praise.

"Chitchat is all well and good," muttered J, "but would someone care to tell me where we're headed, like? If those fellers are comin' after us, it'd be nice to know, because I for one could do with somefing to eat and some shut-eye."

Thaddeus moved to look out over the darkened

landscape. They were flying over dense jungle, the moonlight strong but not enough to show them any safe landing spots. "Our map is still back in that clearing where they attacked us," he said, "and I don't know this area at all. Desai, can you help?"

His friend frowned. "Well, let me see. What direction did we take out of the palace, J?"

J leaned forward and tapped the compass on the control panel. "I headed due north."

"North," Desai repeated thoughtfully. "In that case, yes — I have a very good place for us to head for. Turn her west, J, and follow that heading until you see a river. Once we see that below us, we follow it to its source. It shouldn't be far to fly in this magnificent machine."

"You think that'll be far enough to stop them finding us?" Thaddeus asked.

Desai smiled a little mysteriously. "They may find us, my dear Thaddeus. But I guarantee they will not be able to reach us."

{Chapter 8}

THE PAST
RESURFACES

$\mathcal{H}$ours later, the airship flew toward a huge rock plateau. It rose out of the jungle, a monolith that seemed to have been formed with one strike of an invisible hand. The dawn swarmed around it as the sun rose, vivid streaks of jagged pink and yellow reaching toward them from the horizon. The jungle clustered dense and dark around its base, but on top of the flat rock there was only scrub.

"There," said Desai, pointing. "That should do, don't you think?"

Thaddeus had taken over the controls from J some time earlier, and now he gently brought the airship into land. It bumped slightly on the uneven ground before coming to a rest, sitting on top of the world.

"Best let the balloon down for a bit," suggested J, leaning over Thaddeus's shoulder. "It's probably a bit windy out there, innit? Don't want 'er takin' off without our say-so, like."

"I don't suppose we are going to find any rabbits up here," Rémy said ruefully, absently rubbing her sore neck as she looked out at the sparse foliage that spread over the plateau. There was barely anything higher than a dandelion, and the grass was scrubby. "I am having trouble remembering the last thing we ate . . ."

"Don't worry," Dita told her, "I checked — we still have some rice left, and plenty of water. There's enough for all of us to have some breakfast, anyway. I will set the fire now, yes?"

"Rice for breakfast," J muttered. "It ain't right, I tell yer."

"All right then," shot back Dita, defiant hands on her hips in a pose they had all become used to over the months. "I suppose that means I can have your share?"

"'Ere, that's not what I said! Did you hear me say that? I didn't say that!" J called after her as the girl helped Desai drop the ramp and then disappeared outside, ignoring him.

Rémy left Thaddeus and J to secure the airship and followed the others down the ramp. Outside, there was indeed a brisk wind whipping across the flat rock — to be expected of somewhere so high. Rémy walked to the edge of the plateau, looking out over the vast morass of jungle beneath them. The river they had followed glinted in the rising sun, the water tripping and jumping in flurries of sapphire blue and marble white as it rushed along its haphazard course.

She rubbed her neck again — it was almost as if the ghost of the jeweled man's grip was still clamped around her throat. Rémy had underestimated him — she'd dismissed him as a dandy fop who was all glitter and no substance, easy for her to outwit or outrun. But he had hidden speed and true brute strength beneath those elegant clothes. It had shaken her. She'd felt helpless, and she didn't like it. Little Bird was not used to feeling helpless.

"Penny for them?" Thaddeus's voice floated over her shoulder, and she turned to find him standing behind her. He held a shawl in both hands, reaching out to drape it around her shoulders.

"Oh, nothing," she said, pulling the woolen garment close around her. After the relentless heat it was strange to feel a chill. "Thank you."

Thaddeus rubbed a hand lightly across her back with a smile. He squinted slightly as he looked out into the bright beginning of the day. "What an amazing place. Desai's right: even if they manage to follow us, they'll never make it up here."

"It is a good place to regroup, for sure," agreed Rémy.

"Are you all right?" Thaddeus pulled her closer, running the fingers of one hand along her jaw as he cupped her face with the other and gently tipped her head back to better see the marks on her neck. "For a second there I really thought he might . . ."

Rémy reached up and grasped both his wrists. "Yes. But he did not. And you got me out of there, Thaddeus Rec. Something else for which I should thank you, yes?"

Thaddeus tugged Rémy against him and wrapped his arms around her, her head against his chest. They were silent for a moment, looking out at the landscape that was unfurling before them.

"What if," Rémy asked slowly, "they have something that can help them get up here?"

"What do you mean?"

She pulled back and looked at him. "The jeweled man. He must have the Sapphire Cutlass, must he not?

It is too much of a coincidence, everything that has happened. We know that the Sapphire Cutlass, whatever it is, was somehow behind all those devices that the Comte de Cantal had in his mountain. So what if he has something similar here? What if they are on their way here, right now, with some insane machine that can climb mountains like a goat or — or fly, like the airship?"

Thaddeus frowned thoughtfully, the last shadows of dawn dancing across his face. "That's a good point. Although I don't think he can possibly have anything that flies or why would he want our airship? And that place seemed so dilapidated, when you got really close to it . . . It didn't seem as if he had much to show, let alone much to hide, did it?"

"True," Rémy agreed. She stood on tiptoe to look over Thaddeus's shoulder to where Desai was helping Dita cook the rice. "I think there's only one person here who can tell us what we want to know."

Thaddeus kept one arm around her as he turned to look in the same direction. "I think you're probably right."

Desai got to his feet as they approached, a faint smile on his face. "My friends," he said, his melodic voice dancing in the wind. "I owe you a great debt of gratitude for freeing me as you did — for being here at all, in fact. I still cannot quite believe you came here from England to find me, as Rémy said."

"Actually we came from France," Rémy told him and then, when a look of puzzlement passed Desai's face, added, "but that is a long story and I think we would all prefer to hear yours first."

Desai smiled. "Yes, indeed. Let us sit here as a new day begins, and I will tell you everything. It, too, is a long story — longer than any of you will realize. Please sit."

Rémy took the shawl from around her shoulders and spread it on the ground so that she and Thaddeus could share it. J appeared from the airship, carrying bowls for the rice that was now bubbling steadily in a pot over the flames.

"Ooh," said J, "story time, is it? 'Ang on a tick, I want to hear this, too." The boy set down the bowls and sat beside Dita.

Desai stared at the flames, flickering in the pale light of the rising dawn. "Well, now. Do you remember, my friends, how we first met?"

"Come off it," said J, making a sound in his throat. "We ain't likely to forget somefing like that now, are we?" The boy shuddered. "Although I s'pose the

Little Miss here wasn't there. We was all down in Lord Abernathy's tunnels, see," he told Dita. "Horrible, terrible place, that was. Right under London. 'E was using slaves to build an army to attack the city with. 'E 'ad contraptions down there you wouldn't believe, like."

Dita's eyes grew large and round as she listened mutely.

Desai smiled. "Indeed. But my question was really meant for Miss Brunel," he said softly, looking at her with eyes that were at once kind and full of more knowledge than she could possibly imagine. "Do you remember what I told you then, about the circumstances of your birth, and the curse that your parents passed on to you?"

Rémy nodded, feeling the familiar tingle that always passed up her spine when she thought about everything that Desai had explained to her about her parents. "Of course," she said. "They stole a diamond from a very powerful raja. He had his court magicians place the curse on them, and they passed it on to me when I was born. But what does that have to do with . . . Unless . . . unless . . ." she trailed off, suddenly stunned as the implication of what Desai seemed to be suggesting sank in.

"Yes," the older man said softly. "Did I not say then that it was strange, how the universe conspires to throw us all together, again and again? The man you refer to as the jeweled man is called Ikshuvaku. He was the owner of the diamond your parents stole, Rémy Brunel. The palace from which we have just escaped is where they performed for him, seventeen years ago."

Rémy stood, agitated. "But how can that be so? You said then that he was a rich and powerful leader," she protested. "This man does not seem that way at all. He has jewels, yes — but the palace is crumbling around him, and most of his men are armed only with swords. They do not even have enough rifles to go around all their troops."

Desai was nodding before she had even finished speaking. "It is true. He is not the raja he once was, though he would still dearly love to think of himself as such — which is, of course, what makes him so very dangerous."

"Seventeen years ago: 1857," Thaddeus said thoughtfully. "Rémy had her seventeenth birthday as we journeyed here. I remember that you said she was an Indian baby — conceived here, if not born here. I didn't believe that you could know that just by looking at her, but . . ."

The older man smiled. "Ah, yes. So many significant things occurred in that year — for all of us."

"The Indian Rebellion," Thaddeus added. "That was 1857 as well, wasn't it? Is that why the palace looks as if it was in a great battle? Was this raja — this Ikshuvaku — part of the uprising?"

Desai looked at Thaddeus with amusement. "Again, you surprise me, Thaddeus Rec. I had forgotten what an excellently sharp mind you have behind those curiously colored eyes. The Indian Rebellion took place much farther north — but it sent ripples through the whole continent. It gave men like Ikshuvaku a reason to hope that the grip of the East India Company — and therefore the British Empire itself — could be shaken, and it gave the East India Company a reason to clamp down on anyone they considered troublesome, before they could indeed become so."

"You were here, weren't you?" Rémy said, sitting down again and feeling Thaddeus's hand stroke across her back. "So was Abernathy. You told us that you tried to be a go-between for the British and the raja, to keep the peace. That's why you knew the place and the people so well. Isn't it?"

"That is true indeed, Rémy Brunel. I made several trips to the raja's palace on behalf of the British government." Desai shifted a little uncomfortably, staring into the fire. "What I did not tell you was that during one of those visits, it also became my home."

"What do you mean?" Rémy asked.

"Sahoj sensed my powers — the ones I had kept hidden from the colonials. He knew my abilities could assist Ikshuvaku's cause. So they flattered me, and over time I . . . allowed myself to be flattered. I chose to switch my allegiance. I stayed and became one of the court's mystics, in Sahoj's circle. For a time it was wonderfully freeing to exercise skills that few others possess. For a time I was treated like royalty myself, and, I am ashamed to admit, I reveled in it. But by the time the British attacked, I had been banished from the palace walls."

"Why?" J asked, listening closely even as he held out their bowls one by one for Dita to ladle rice into. "What did you do?"

"It was what I didn't do, young man, as much as what I did." Desai sighed, as if raking over the memories of those distant years was painful. "I told you the court mystics were ordered to put a curse on your parents, Rémy. I was one of them — and I refused. I did not think your parents or their unborn children deserved such a fate. Gustave was a different matter, and had that been the only order I would not have hesitated as I did.

"But in any case it made no difference. I was not the only mystic with such power, and no one else objected. The curse was set without me, by a man called Sahoj, who had always been more reckless with his powers than I, and less compassionate in the use of them. My disobedience was the start of my downfall.

"When Ikshuvaku began to make plans to rise up against the British, I knew I could not stand by or, worse, help. I could see that it would be a disaster — Ikshuvaku always did overestimate his strength. An uprising would be crushed, and brutally, it was clear. The northern rebellions had had the advantage of surprise, but the Company was prepared now, and on the lookout. He himself might survive, but the people — the poor, the desperate — whom he planned to press into his army would not. I tried to convince him not to act, but by then I was an object of mistrust. They labeled me a traitor and threw me out. By that time, relations between the raja and the British were completely sour anyway, thanks in part to Abernathy. The diamond he recovered from your parents was not the only one he stole. He took many of the Raja's lesser jewels. Not that it did him any good — when the East India Company found out, they tried him as a looter because he had not turned his spoils over to the crown. He was thrown into jail."

"An' that's where 'e met the Professor!" J realized.

"Yes, J, that is where he met our hapless friend, the Professor. And so our paths were set, all those years ago. The rest you know."

"Not everything," Thaddeus said. "How did you end up back there, and as a prisoner?"

Desai sighed. "A year ago, when I returned with the diamond in order to lift Rémy's curse once and for all, it was the first time I had approached Ikshuvaku since being banished. I was unsure of what reception I would receive, though I was sure he would welcome the return of the jewel, if nothing else. I knew from the eyes and ears I still had here that he had fallen on hard times — the uprising had indeed been stamped out with a harsh foot." He paused, spooning up a mouthful of rice and chewing silently, seeming to be miles away, his face lined with sadness.

After a moment he went on. "I found the place changed, but still recognizable. The intervening years had been difficult, but Ikshuvaku's spirit had not been extinguished. Once the seeds of rebellion had been drowned, the British had left him alone: they rightly thought he was no longer a threat. He was older and — I thought, anyway — wiser . . . I left to return to London with my spirits buoyed. My only concern was the influence that Sahoj still seemed to hold over both Ikshuvaku and his court at large. I asked my eyes and ears at the palace to keep me apprised of proceedings. For a while all was well. Then I got word that Sahoj had persuaded Ikshuvaku to do something very stupid. So I came back once again, and tried to talk Ikshuvaku out of this insanity. And I have been a prisoner ever since."

"And what was that?" Thaddeus asked. "What was it that Sahoj had persuaded Ikshuvaku to do that was so stupid?"

Desai put down his bowl and rubbed one hand across his forehead. "Sahoj had decided," he said quietly, "to wake the Sapphire Cutlass."

"But what is that?" Rémy asked. "What *is* the Sapphire Cutlass?"

Desai turned, his eyes glittering with a dark light. "It is not a *what*, Rémy Brunel. It is a *she*."

{Chapter 9}

A SORRY TALE

"Well, who is she?" Thaddeus asked. "How is it that you are so afraid of her? Is she a queen of some sort? With an army?"

"No, she is not a queen," said Desai quietly. "She is not even a servant. She is an Untouchable, the lowest of the low . . . or at least, she was, once. She may still be, yet. I have never seen her. Indeed, I do not believe she really exists."

Thaddeus frowned. "I think you're going to have to explain a little more," he told Desai, "because, I'm sorry, but I for one just do not understand."

The older man smiled somewhat sadly. The dawn light was becoming almost blinding. The sun had risen over the horizon and was casting glaring rays across the landscape, silhouetting Desai where he sat. He looked into a glare for a moment, and then nodded.

"To truly explain," he began, "I must go back a long way. Back beyond the time, even, of the first men, back to when the Earth first came into being. There are many gods, great and small, some good and some not so good, and when they saw the beauty and bounty of India, they all wanted it for themselves. The gods dislike to war among themselves — why else would they make the Earth, if not to people it with beings who could fight amongst themselves in their place? And so the great gods divided it into pieces, amicably. And these pieces they gave to their foot soldiers: stewards they trusted to ensure that the affairs of Earth were kept in order. Spirits, some might call them. Angels, others."

"'Ang about a bit," J interjected, a look of puzzlement on his face. "Is this stuff all real now, Mr. Desai? Cos I 'ave to tell you, I ain't never believed in angels, no matter what the Sally Ann tried to tell me."

Desai smiled at the boy. "That, my dear J, is something you will have to decide for yourself. I am merely telling the story the way I know how to tell it. How you decide to hear it is your own affair. Did you not learn of many things that caused you to wonder during our last visit?"

"Tha's true," admitted J. "Whenever I wasn't roastin' from the 'eat I was lookin' at somefing extraordinary, an' that's no mistake."

"Well, then," said his mentor, "let us continue, and see what you make of this particular wonder. So the land was divided up into pieces, and populated accordingly. The land was bountiful and beautiful, and the foot soldiers of the gods found ways to provide amply for the people who found it their home — fish to the people near the seas and rivers, meat to those farther inland, rice to the plains and hills in between. They created so much variety that the gods became jealous of their skill, and commanded them to cease. Whatever was in existence on that day would be the extent of creation. There must be no more. The gods decreed it. This caused no trouble for most of them — there had been such a flurry of invention that most sections of the land teemed with creatures of great beauty, and each place had been given something unique with which to trade for those things that they did not have.

"But for one of them, it was not enough. He had been given this land, here — this strip that stretches inland from the ocean — and he cared about the people who dwelt within the borders he had been commanded to protect. He had spent so much time perfecting the land that he had failed to provide anything unique with which his people could trade. They had some fish from the waters, and they had some game from the creatures that wandered across their land. But he wanted them to have something that was purely their own — something secret and valuable that would secure their future as long as they tended it wisely.

"He petitioned the gods for more time, but they were adamant. They would give no more. Creation was set, and the people must do what they could with what they had. The foot soldier must leave them be and return to his place with the gods. The people must fend for themselves. Angry and distressed, the spirit became a tower of sheer strength, a glittering giant who reflected the flawless blue of the sky. Incensed beyond reason, he stamped his foot, and in his rage he struck the nails of his toes against the great rocks of the land. They shattered, and the shards plunged into the ground, tearing it up into a mountain, hidden in a deep valley formed by the shape of his foot, far from any place that it could be easily reached or found.

The shards of his nails, stained blue from the sky, became jewels buried in the Earth. And so, in his fury, the spirit had found a way to provide for his people. A single mountain, veined with stones the color of a perfect sky, to be mined only by the people within his borders."

"Blue stones the color of the sky," murmured Rémy. "Sapphires. You are talking about sapphires, are you not?"

Desai smiled. "Sapphires indeed, Rémy Brunel, oh great knower of gems. He gave his people the only sapphire mine in the south of this great continent, to be kept a secret for eternity, mined only by the villages that were in the valley around the mountain. They would take only what they needed in order to trade, and no stranger would ever be allowed within its confines."

"I suppose we know that that did not happen," said Dita. "Or you would not know about it now, *ja?*"

"You are quite right, of course, Miss Dita. For centuries the mine remained secret. The sapphires that were taken from it were flawless, peerless — more valuable, even, than the great diamonds of Golconda. Some rulers, over the years, did try to find their source, but they never succeeded."

"So what happened?" Thaddeus asked.

"The world came to India," Desai told them. "Hundreds of years ago, when the Portuguese walked onto this land, a young man of their number decided to make a name for himself by uncovering sights that no person from his country had seen before. He traveled far and wide, and in doing so stumbled across the hidden valley of the sapphire mountain. The villagers, having never been visited by foreigners before, were curious and invited him to stay for a while.

"The family that took him in had a young daughter, Aruna. This daughter was beautiful and as bright as the jewels she worked with her father and brothers to mine. The young man was dazzled by her, and she by him. The village elders were careful not to tell this stranger of their mine, but soon he became curious as to where all the able-bodied went every day. He persuaded the girl to tell him, and thereafter became obsessed with the idea of the riches this mine represented, and the glory he would garner for revealing it to the outside world.

"He asked Aruna to be his wife, believing that as her husband he would be able to trade the sapphires in the mine more profitably. Aruna loved him, and believed his intentions to be pure. The village elders, though, were suspicious, and they forbade the match. The Portuguese man left the village, telling Aruna that he could not yet afford to keep a wife, but that he would return for her when he could.

"Aruna, having begged and pleaded with the village elders to no avail, grew sick with longing. She loved her family and her village, but she loved the young man more. She feared that he would not come back — that he would forget her entirely. And so she decided that if he could not afford to keep her, she would have to keep herself. She would steal from the mine — not a lot, just enough to pay her way through the world and marry her love.

"The very next day, while deep in the mine, Aruna concealed two small sapphires in her mouth, so as to smuggle them out as she left that evening. She waited until that night, when her family was asleep, and then left the village. It was only when she reached the nearest town and tried to retrieve the sapphires to sell that Aruna realized she had swallowed one of the stones. Though an annoyance, she thought nothing of it — she sold the one remaining stone, which was enough to take her to Pondicherry, where the Portuguese had told her he was headed when he left. On the journey, she began to feel a great pain in her stomach, but she carried on, buoyed up by the belief that she was about to be reunited with her one true love.

"When she got to Pondicherry, she expected to be welcomed with open arms. But instead, she found her lover at the head of a garrison of soldiers, preparing as if for war. At the sight of her, he shrugged and told her she was no longer needed. Aruna was forced to watch as the garrison set off, by now too sick to follow.

"For days she was in pain and unable to move. She was taken in by a kindly couple who let her stay with them. There she remained, sick in heart and in body, until one day a great commotion rose to her sickbed from the street outside. Aruna dragged herself to the window and saw below the garrison led by the young man, returned. And each horse was laden with a sack, crammed with the most beautiful sapphires anyone had ever seen.

"At the sight, a rage overtook Aruna, for she knew exactly where these blue stones had come from. Her fury blotted out her pain, and she rushed from the house to confront the Portuguese man. He looked upon her with fear, and Aruna looked down to see that her nails had become talons of clear, pure sapphire. First she divested him of his curved sword, the cutlass that would later become her moniker and the symbol of her revenge. Then she tore him apart with her bare hands. Still enraged, she fled back to her home village.

"The village no longer stood. It had been razed by the Portuguese soldiers, every one of Aruna's family and friends put to the sword for refusing to give up the mountain. They were all dead, thanks to the love of one girl and the greed of one man.

"Aruna's fury mingled with a grief so potent that it drew storms from the sky. She stood, raging and hateful of the world, until a bolt of lightning struck the cutlass she still carried. Its energy surged through Aruna, finding the sapphire still within her belly, seeking it as surely as a plant seeks the sun.

"The stone within her, already woken by grief and shame and anger, came alive. It raged within her belly, pouring its ancient wisdom into the woman's body, flooding her veins with more than fury — filling her with a power so great that it rivaled the storms above her head. She turned on the Portuguese garrison who had come to avenge their comrades' deaths, tearing them apart, pummeling their flesh to ribbons in the space of time that it would take a mortal to draw breath. Her rampage did not burn itself out — she flew onward through the jungles, killing wherever she found life, so full of hatred that she was blind to her victims, seeing only her lover's face.

"Her fury was such that the gods themselves were woken from their slumber. They saw that with the power of the sapphire, this woman could become one of their number. They sent a group of wise men the means to subdue her into a sleep as great as their own. Aruna was placed deep inside the mountain from whence both her grief and her power originated, never again to walk the Earth. The valley of the mountain was cursed so that no one would ever again willingly set foot in its jungles. Over the years, the story has changed shape many times. There are people who admire Aruna for her strength, and worship her for her power. There are people who have made her a symbol of hope — a goddess for the downtrodden and mistreated. But no one has ever gone so far as to speak of waking her again."

"Until now," murmured Rémy.

"Yes," said Desai, with a somber sigh that seemed to draw a thread of darkness through the bright tapestry of the new day. "Until now."

Chapter 10

A NEW CULT

"But — but this is just a fable," protested Thaddeus into the silence that had fallen following Desai's tale. "It's just a story — it can't be true!"

"Surely by now you must realize, my dear Thaddeus, that what is true has far less importance than what is believed," said Desai. "Besides, do you doubt that gemstones can wield great powers? After what you saw in Abernathy's tunnels — after your means of travel from one side of the Earth to the other?" He gestured at the airship.

Thaddeus nodded. It was true — however rationally he thought about it, he could not deny the evidence of his own eyes. "And what do *you* believe, Desai?" he asked.

Desai looked back at him, his expression deadly serious. "That whatever kernel of truth is in the story is irrelevant. It is the cult that has grown up around the tale that is the true danger."

"A cult?" Rémy repeated. "You mean there are still people who worship the idea of Aruna and her power?"

"Absolutely there are," said Desai, "and as with all faith, it only takes a clever mind to manipulate such devotion. For centuries these people have kept themselves secret — but now their numbers are swelling. They believe that Aruna is about to rise again, and they are flocking to serve her — or whomever has designated themselves her mouthpiece — while they still can."

"Someone is encouraging them?" asked Thaddeus, and he was rewarded by a nod from Desai.

"Just so. This, I think, is Sahoj's most clever plan. Hidden away in Aruna's mountain, he is building an army, and he has not even had to recruit them. They are coming to him."

"Sahoj," repeated Rémy. "When I was finding my

way into the palace, I saw Ikshuvaku speak with an old man dressed in white robes. Is this who you mean?"

"Indeed it is," said Desai.

"He did not seem happy by the capture of the airship," Rémy observed.

Desai gave a brief smile. "I imagine the idea of the raja having any strength at his own command plays against whatever Sahoj is planning," he said. "It would suit him best to have the raja dependent on his power."

"But what could he be planning?" Thaddeus asked. "Another uprising against the British?"

Desai shook his head. "If that were all he were interested in, I would not be as concerned as I am. Unfortunately, even if the tale about reawakening the girl is false, the powers of the stones in those mines are true. If Sahoj has found a way to channel that power — as I believe he must at least *think* he has, or he would not be so audacious — then we must all fear the outcome, for I have no doubt his ambitions will extend far beyond these shores.

"But most frightening of all is that he may believe he can control the power he has sought out — he may even succeed, for a time — but sooner or later he will fail. What is in that mountain was not meant to exist and its power cannot be safely harnessed, much less wielded. This is what the fable of the Sapphire Cutlass is intended to show. We must find a way to stop him, before the cult and its notoriety spreads. For the more it does so, the greater Sahoj's confidence will be."

Thaddeus and Rémy shared an uncomfortable look, which did not go unnoticed by Desai.

"What is it?" he asked. "My young friends, if you have something to say, I beg you — speak."

Thaddeus straightened his shoulders with a sigh. "I don't know how to tell you this, Desai, but I think it has already spread beyond India."

"Go on," the older man said.

"We told you we came here from France, yes?" Rémy said gently.

"Quite. I was going to ask you about that, in due course."

"You will remember that before you left on your journey here, you visited me in my office at the station and gave me a list of names," added Thaddeus. "On that list was the Comte de Cantal. It was he who took us to France."

As quickly as he could — and with help from Rémy, J, and Dita — Thaddeus outlined the events that had surrounded the destruction of Mount Cantal. As the story unfolded — the kidnap of Claudette and Amélie, their discovery that the Comte's entire mountain had been turned into a factory for a huge mechanical army — Desai's face grew darker and darker. He stared into the distance, listening intently.

"The thing is," Thaddeus went on, almost hesitant to reveal the crux of the matter, "the thing is, Desai, that when he was leading me through that volcano, he revealed that he knew Abernathy. Or at least, if he did not know him personally, then he knew of him. He spoke of warning someone that Abernathy was not ready to receive the power he had obtained. And I saw, on his breast, a tattoo. It was of a curved sword, with a hilt inlaid with a sapphire embedded in his skin."

Silence reigned for a moment, punctuated by nothing but the dying crackle of the fire and the call of the jungle birds, waking into the day.

"It cannot be a coincidence, I think, what Thaddeus saw?" Rémy prompted, after a moment or two.

Desai shook his head. "No, it cannot. That motif matches the symbol of the Sapphire Cutlass, for sure. Their followers see it as proof of their devotion to tattoo themselves accordingly."

"Then," said Thaddeus hesitantly, "are we to assume — my god, Desai — are we to assume that all of those names on the list you gave me are members of this cult? They were spread all over the world, weren't they? I remember names from as distant as the Far East on that piece of paper!"

Desai nodded, his mouth a thin, hard line. "From what you have told me, and what you have discovered, I fear you must be correct."

He got to his feet, agitated, and began to pace. "I have tarried too long. I have been arrogant. I came to India imagining that I could deal with this problem on my own — that it was a thing I could contain by myself, as if Ikshuvaku and Sahoj were merely errant children. But I am too late. Perhaps it was too late before I even set foot on my homeland. If there are threads from the Sapphire Cutlass already sewn throughout the world, perhaps there is nothing more to be done. Perhaps there never was."

Thaddeus got to his feet, dusting his hands off on his trousers. "That can't be true. I won't accept it. We defeated both Abernathy and Cantal. Perhaps we still have a chance to do something, if we act now. Do you have any idea what might stop this, Desai?"

Desai spread his hands. "My young friends, I do not. But whatever is to be done — if anything can be — the doing of it must take place within that mountain."

"Where is it, then?" J asked. "Is it a long way away, like? Cos I'm willin' to wager that this beastie has been farther, Mr. Desai." He waved proudly at the airship.

The older man smiled and said, "In some ways, it is very close, J, and in others it is a lifetime away." He raised his arm and swept it out over the horizon, which now glowed in the bright yellow sunlight of an Indian day. He pointed, and there in the distance, silhouetted against the light, reached the jagged tip of a twisted mountain, its lower reaches plunging into a valley so deep and so clogged with jungle that from where they stood, as high as the plateau was, it proved impossible to see from whence the mountain sprung.

"There," said Desai. "There is the mountain created by the angry stamp of a lesser god, and there lie the answers to the questions we have posed for ourselves."

"Right, then," said J, getting to his feet and slapping his hands against his thighs. "Well, what are we waiting here for then? Places to be, things to do. Let's be 'avin' you, eh?"

"J, it is not that simple," cautioned Desai.

"Why ain't it? There it is, right there, and you's said that's where we got to go to work this fing out. So I say we hop to it, quick like, before this Sahoj and his Sapphire wotsit 'as a chance to see us comin'."

"J, I know what a brave soul you are. I know what brave souls you all are," said Desai, his words encompassing the whole of their small assembly. "But this is not what we found in Abernathy's lair. It is not even what you encountered in France. This is on a different scale, and what we find there . . . What we find there could well be the end of everything we know. Think of the legend of Aruna. Think of those soldiers, torn apart by the bare hands of an unarmed young girl. Think what sort of power could induce such events as that."

There was a brief silence, which Thaddeus broke in a soft, but firm, voice. "Well then," he said, "that's all the more reason for us to hurry. Wouldn't you say, Desai?"

Desai looked at him, and then at each of their faces in turn. Something passed through his eyes — an emotion so large that even their dark depths struggled to contain it. He seemed to struggle to speak for a moment, and when he did his voice was thick. "My young friends. Your courage and loyalty are lessons for all. And if you are our future, then perhaps it is in better hands than we even deserve."

"So tha's settled, then," said J. "We're all going. And I say we don't lose any more time chin-wagging, or it'll be time for lunch and frankly, I ain't missing another one o' those unless the sky is fallin' in."

Dita nudged him in the ribs with an elbow. "Be careful what you wish for, eh, dirty boy."

"I keep *tellin'* you," J said, "I ain't —"

"There is one thing," said Desai, his voice cutting through the children's squabbling, "that we must address first."

Thaddeus frowned. "Oh? What's that?"

Desai turned to Rémy with a soft smile. "Your knowledge of the Sapphire Cutlass is not the only thing you brought with you from France, am I right?"

Thaddeus watched as Rémy's face passed from confusion and into realization. "Oh," she said. "Do you mean the puzzle box? But — but that is of no importance, Desai. It can wait."

Desai raised an eyebrow. "Of no importance? This trinket that you risked your life to reclaim from the raja's palace is of no importance?"

"I mean, it is not as important as everything else," Rémy amended. "Anyway, I think the thing does not work at all. We have all tried for months to open it and we cannot."

Their friend smiled. "My dear, I am inclined to believe that where you are concerned at least, there is

very little that is not important. In this case, I am sure
of it. May I ask what you believe it to contain?"

Rémy sighed. "An old woman, in France — a medi-
cine woman — she gave it to me. She told me it would
take me to the truth. She was also the one who told
me that I had a brother: a twin, born just before me.
I thought she meant the truth about my brother. But
maybe I'm wrong about what she meant. Or she may
just have been crazy — and anyway, if I have never
known him yet, it cannot matter if I never do at all."

"Do you really believe that?" Desai asked.

Rémy shrugged, twining her fingers together restlessly. "*Monsieur*, what can it matter that I may have a
brother if the fate of the world is in the balance?"

Desai smiled. "What indeed. May I see it?"

Rémy hesitated for a moment and then crossed to
where her leather bag sat on the ground. Pulling it
open, she fished in its depths for the cube, then passed
it to Desai. He turned it around in his hands, watching
the play of sunlight dance across the intricate whorls
and patterns on each surface. Then he looked up at
her.

"You trust me with this?"

"I — yes, of course. I trust all of you. I would not
have shown it to anyone but Thaddeus, otherwise."

Desai nodded with a slightly sad smile. "It is a balm to a weary soul such as mine, Rémy Brunel, to find such optimism in one who has endured such hardships as you."

Rémy blinked. "I am not —" She trailed off as Desai gripped the box in both hands. Instead of attempting to open the stubborn hinges, as they had each tried in turn, he held it out in front of him and twisted, one hand moving right and one hand moving left.

Rémy watched, astonished, as the box realigned itself, shearing smoothly along the new angle offered it by Desai. Still the hinges did not open, but they did fold in on themselves. A moment later, where once the box had been a perfect cube, now it was a sphere formed of triangles. Desai held out his hand, the newly formed sphere resting on his palm. As they all watched, a feature appeared on its uppermost curve — a button, clicking out of the whole.

"It is yours to press, Rémy Brunel," said Desai quietly.

Holding her breath, Rémy stepped forward and hesitantly reached out a hand. The box was gleaming as if lit from inside, which she knew to be nonsense — it was merely the gold of its outer shell refracting the sun's bright rays. The sphere felt warm to the touch, as if it had been woken, somehow, from a deep, deep sleep.

She pressed the button. It pushed in with a sharp click, and then — almost before Rémy could move her hand away — the sphere began to react. Each of the triangles that formed one half of the sphere flicked outward, until they stood open like the petals of a flower.

Inside was a compass. With trembling fingers, Rémy reached in and lifted it out.

Chapter 11

THE PUZZLE
UNDONE

The others all moved closer to see. The compass seemed very old — a hand-painted dial set in a glass-faced gold case with two filigree hands pointing north and south that looked almost too delicate for their task. Rémy held the device in her hand, and as she did so, something on the dial began to move. A tiny flap opened and a fold of gold popped up through it. It didn't seem to be affixed to anything, but instead wavered for a few seconds, whisking up and down the arc that represented north and south. Then it stopped, turned around on itself once, and began to unfurl. As they all watched, a third hand, smaller than the first two and even more delicate, unrolled out of itself like the frond of a new fern. It wriggled for a moment or two in its new state before setting firm.

"Cripes," said J, after a moment of silence as they all continued to watch the compass, waiting to see if it would do anything else. "I ain't never seen nothin' like that."

"Do you know what this is, Rémy?" Desai asked quietly.

Rémy shook her head, still staring at the compass in her hand, transfixed. "No, *monsieur*. Like J, I have never seen such a thing. I am sure that none of us have. Except maybe you, of course?"

Desai nodded and then, being careful not to touch the compass, pointed to the new hand. "You see this? This is your direction, Rémy. This is the direction you must follow."

She looked up at him with a frown. "What do you mean?"

"You will find your truth — and possibly, with it, your twin brother — on this bearing. Moreover, you must follow it immediately, for the third arm will lose its direction as the sun sets on the day it is activated." He paused and looked up at the sky, into which the new sun was gleaming joyfully. "You are lucky, Rémy Brunel. Today will last a long time."

"But — wait," said Rémy, her mind spinning. "I — I cannot follow it now. We — we must help you deal with the Sapphire Cutlass first."

Desai smiled at her gently. "No, my dear girl, I do not believe that is your true course. If it were, the hand would point toward the mountain, would it not? And see here — it points to the southeast, which is very nearly in the opposite direction."

"But — no," said Rémy, still perplexed. "I cannot follow it, then. Not now."

"If you don't, you will lose your chance to know the truth."

"I — I will take a note of the new heading, and follow it another time," said Rémy, shrugging with a nonchalance she didn't feel. Her stomach was churning, her heart beating in an unsteady patter. *"D'accord?* I have promised to help you, Desai, and Rémy Brunel does not abandon her promises so easily."

Desai smiled again and reached out to take her arm in a firm but gentle grip. "There is a reason the heading only lasts for a day, Rémy. Tomorrow the truth — or at least where it is situated — will be different. If you do not follow it, you may never find it at all."

"But — but I don't even know if this is about my brother!" Rémy exclaimed, frustrated and infuriated, though she didn't really know why. "It could be about anything!"

"Indeed, that could be true," Desai said, a gentle smile still in his eyes. "But somehow, I think not. Boxes such as these are rare, Rémy, and to find them gifted even rarer. Be honest with me now. What do you think most about these days? What have you thought most about since you arrived here, in India, the place where you know you were conceived?"

Rémy couldn't help looking at Thaddeus. He was watching her with eyes that, though they were shadowed with worry, were still full of the gentle reassurance she always saw there when she took the time to look. He smiled at her, and she wanted to say that she had spent most of her time thinking about him — which was almost true, or would have been if something else hadn't always been lurking in the back of her mind.

"To find out about my family," she said softly, still looking at Thaddeus. "To — to find out if I really do have a brother."

"Quite," said Desai, dropping his arm with another smile. "This is enough to tell me that the truth you seek — the truth that is indicated along that heading — is about exactly that."

"You knew," she said. "You knew what was going to be inside the puzzle box. Why would you have me open it now, when there are so many more things to worry about? How can I go and follow my own path when there is so much that needs to be done?"

"You imagine that these things are unconnected, Rémy Brunel," Desai told her. "But you are the common thread that has run through this story from start to finish, and I cannot believe that your twin is not a similar part of the weft and weave. If we are nearing this tapestry's completion, it seems to me that if you can find him, it is of as much importance to the pattern as anything else we may encounter from here on."

"He's right," Thaddeus said softly, stepping closer. "After all, if you do have a brother and if he's even half as wonderful as you are, Rémy Brunel — well, I for one would like him by my side in whatever fight may be coming."

Rémy looked down at the compass, still resting patiently in her palm. "How far will I have to go?" she asked Desai, her voice rasping against her suddenly dry throat. "How long will it take?"

"I don't know," Desai told her. "These, too, are truths that will only be revealed along the way."

"Take the airship," J piped up. "You've sailed it yerself enough to know 'ow to handle 'er, Rémy. That'll speed things up, eh?"

"I can't do that — if everything you have told us is really so, Desai, you will need it, yes? You will need to be able to escape quickly."

Desai shook his head. "Arriving by air will draw too much attention. We must use stealth from here on. Besides, Sahoj has seen it, has he not? He'll be looking for it. Better that he does not see it coming. You can fly us as far as the farthest reaches of the valley and drop us there. That way we may even fool him a little — make him think we have contemplated entering the valley and turned back out of fear, as many a person has before. Any small advantage we can garner will be a help of incalculable worth."

"But — but —" Rémy looked from one to the other, until her gaze rested on Thaddeus, who, with a smile, reached out to pull her into a soft embrace. Rémy turned her head so that it rested against his chest. The others moved away, leaving them to it.

For a few minutes they said nothing, only held each other. Then Thaddeus pulled back slightly and Rémy raised her head to look at him.

"You have to go," he told her. "You know you do, Rémy."

"I'd be leaving you again," she murmured. "I promised myself last time that I would never do that again."

"I told you — I'll come with you. Whatever's out there, Rémy, we'll face it together."

She shook her head. "You can't come with me, Thaddeus. You heard what Desai said, about what could be waiting in that mountain. He will need all the help he can get — J and Dita won't be enough, you know that. If I really am to go — then you must stay."

Thaddeus thought for a moment, his eyes scanning the horizon over her head. Eventually he sighed and nodded. "You're right, of course."

"I wish I'd never opened the box," Rémy said miserably. "I wish I'd left it to the raja, and good riddance. I don't want to leave you. I don't want to leave any of you, but you most of all, Thaddeus Rec."

Thaddeus smiled and pressed a kiss to her forehead. "You'll be back. You and I — we're like that compass of yours," he said, nodding to where she still held it in one hand. "You're my north, Rémy, and I'm the arrow that points to you. We'll always swing back toward each other in the end."

He kissed her again, this time on the lips so that her words died away amid a blur of happiness tinged with worry and guilt. They parted after a moment, and Thaddeus rested his forehead against hers.

Eventually Rémy looked up at him, still hesitating even as the sun rose higher and higher on her back. As usual, time seemed to be running out, and she wondered how it could always be the case that, however old the universe was and however long it had existed, whenever something important had to be decided, it actually turned out there was no time at all.

"Go," Thaddeus whispered. "There's no choice to make, Rémy. Find this brother of yours and bring him back to fight with us."

She nodded reluctantly, and then, before he had a chance to move away, pushed herself up on tiptoe and kissed him deeply. Thaddeus took her hand as they broke apart, turning to Desai, J, and Dita.

"Let's go," he said.

Desai nodded, striding forward. "It is the right decision, Rémy. The only decision, truly. But now I must ask you for a favor."

"Of course," said Rémy, "I will do anything I can."

"I must ask you for the loan of your opal," said Desai. "I know that it is precious — the only memento you have of your parents. But it is possible that if we are to defeat the Sapphire Cutlass, the stone may be able to help."

Rémy put her hand to her neck, a reflex reaction returning her to an old habit she'd harbored for years. Until just a few months ago, the opal necklace given to her by her mother had been her constant companion, always hanging on a thin gold chain at her throat. But now, beneath her black shirt, her neck was bare.

"I'm so sorry, Desai, but I do not have it. I have not had it for months. I gave it to Claudette, so that she might speak to Amélie . . ."

Desai's face clouded with fresh worry for a moment, before he dispelled it with a wide smile. "Ah, well. It was just a thought. Come, my friends, we must be about our business, and let Miss Brunel be about hers."

Dita and J kicked dust across the remains of the fire as Thaddeus and Rémy readied the airship for flight. Rémy was at the controls as the ship rose into the air, turning her nose to head for the one patch of jungle that steadily refused to be lit by the sun — a valley so steeply banked and so densely packed with foliage that it gave off a darkness greater than that of the night they had so recently left behind.

Far below, weaving swiftly through the thick

undergrowth, a group of soldiers left the great shadow cast by the huge rock monolith. Following on horseback, dressed in turquoise and white, they had watched and waited all night for the airship to leave its safe harbor.

Their patience, it seemed, had finally paid off.

* * *

With fresh gas in the airship's balloon, the journey toward the mountain was a swift one. Desai told Rémy to put down before they reached the valley that stretched away from its foot. It would attract too much attention and be too dangerous, he said, to fly directly into the cult's lair. They chose a small clearing quite some way from the valley's farthest reach, where the sun still dappled the ground instead of refracting off the dense jungle leaves. Desai, Dita, and J took the scant equipment they had chosen and left the airship.

Then all that was left was for Thaddeus to bid Rémy goodbye.

"I hate this," she muttered as he pulled her against his chest. "I should be coming with you."

Thaddeus kissed the top of her head. "Everything will be fine," he told her.

She pulled back and looked up at him. "You cannot possibly know that!"

He smiled. "Don't be such a pessimist."

"Don't be such an idiot," she retorted.

He grinned. "If I wasn't, I don't think you would love me quite as much."

Her eyes gleamed for a second and Thaddeus knew she'd thought of a sharp comeback. He leaned forward and kissed her before she could say it. Rémy wound her arms around his shoulders and when they broke apart, they lingered there, their foreheads touching, until Desai's voice broke the silence.

"My young friends, it pains me to separate you, but we should all be on our way," he said, his gentle voice floating to them from the airship's ramp. "If the landing of the airship was noticed, we do not want to be in the vicinity when someone comes."

Rémy pushed out of Thaddeus's arms with a nod. "Go," she said, "and I will too — the sooner I follow this heading, the sooner I will come back for you all, yes?"

Thaddeus smiled. "Fly safely, Little Bird."

"Do not lose your way, little policeman."

They looked at each other for another moment, and then Thaddeus turned and left. He stood on the jungle's soft earth and watched as Rémy winched the airship's ramp back into place, hiding her from his view inch by inch until she disappeared completely.

Desai placed a hand on his shoulder. "You will see her again, Thaddeus, and soon. I am sure of that."

The airship began to lift off as Thaddeus turned with a smile. "I know I will."

He looked up to see that the airship — and Rémy with it — was already high above the tree line, sailing away into the blue, blue sky.

Chapter 12

AMBUSH

$\mathcal{I}$t had yet to reach nine o'clock in the morning, but the air was already hot. It beat down on the thick, silent jungle, turning the air into a heady, humid soup of smell and sensation. Thaddeus could feel his pack sticking to his back, his shirt already drenched in sweat, though they had barely begun their trek toward the valley. Below his feet, the soft ground was slowly beginning to slope up into the steep pass that marked the valley's entrance from the direction they had chosen. Ahead, he could see the jagged lines of the rise they would have to navigate. It formed a landscape the Englishman had never seen before — a level line of cracked earth through which grew a line of trees so dense that their leaves seemed to gather darkness against their trunks. The trees stood like sentries at their posts: still, impenetrable, forbidding.

The legend was right about one thing. It was not anywhere Thaddeus would have chosen to go willingly.

The somber air seemed to have had a similar effect on his companions. J trailed behind Desai, who had taken the lead. The boy's head was down and his shoulders were slumped. Even J's usually rambunctious hair was subdued, plastered against his scalp in the haze of heat that surrounded them. Dita was quiet for a change, too, no sign of the constant bickering that usually typified her conversations with J. The little girl stared around her, her eyes flicking anxiously here and there as if trying to keep watch on the whole forest around them.

Desai, meanwhile, toiled stoically on ahead, and not for the first time Thaddeus wondered at the man's endurance. Desai must have reached his sixtieth year, and actually had probably surpassed it, but he showed no signs of fatigue or physical distress. Although, the younger man reflected, perhaps that had more to do with what he knew was ahead for them.

Thaddeus, making up the rear, had spent much of his time thinking about Rémy. Her absence now was the first time they had been apart in all the months since their exodus from France, and even though he knew full well where she was and what she was doing, even though they had said goodbye just an hour or so before and he had seen the airship depart, Thaddeus still found himself, in those split-seconds between one thought and the next, looking up and expecting to see her. Her absence simply felt wrong. His body and his mind could not absorb it.

Things had changed between them over those past months. They had become easier, less fraught with misunderstanding and argument. They had got to know each other better, they had become accustomed to each other's moods and daily routines, each other's likes and dislikes. They fitted together better — they fitted together *well*, which wasn't something either of them thought would be possible for two such disparate people.

What did it mean? If they fit so well that even an hour apart felt unnatural and strange, at least at first — what did that *mean*? Affairs of the heart, he reflected, were so much more difficult to navigate than a police investigation.

But he thought he knew. Thaddeus reached into his pocket, finding the tiny object that he had put there weeks ago and frequently taken out to look at since, without ever finding the right time to give it to its intended recipient.

Thaddeus pulled his fingers away from the trinket with a sigh. Of course, being apart may not feel at all odd to Rémy, who was quite possibly the most independent person he knew. It was one of the many things he loved about her, partly because he thought it boded well for him. She didn't need anyone at all, really, and yet still she chose to stick with him.

The sharp snap of a twig brought Thaddeus out of his reverie in a second. The sound had come from behind him, and he turned, surveying the forest for any sign of movement. He could see nothing, but a renewed sense of unease poured fresh tension into his shoulders.

"Desai . . ." he called, keeping his voice low. "I think . . ."

The attack was upon them before he even managed to finish his sentence. Four men clad in the raja's colors appeared from the undergrowth, teeth bared and fists clenched. Thaddeus backed up, keeping his face to them, realizing with a jolt that none of them had drawn their swords.

"They want to take us alive!" Desai shouted. "Do not let them get close enough — make for the valley, as fast as you can!"

Thaddeus saw J grab Dita's hand and together the two children made a run for it. He hung back, hoping to give them a chance to get a head start, but two of the men peeled off from their group and followed them.

Thaddeus began to run himself, dodging under the lowest branches he could find in an attempt to slow down whomever might be on his trail. He saw Desai a little way to his left, doing the same. The men pursuing them were fast and nimble, but one-on-one, even if it came to a fight, they had a chance. He wondered why there were not more of them, and where their horses were. If the raja had sent them, they must have been following the airship and to do that would require —

Of course, he thought, darting around the thin trunk of a tree, *the airship. That's what the raja really wants. If there were more men like these, they will have gone after it. Godspeed, Rémy . . .*

He felt a hand clamp on his shoulder, heavy breathing just behind him as the touch spun him around. Thaddeus ducked under his attacker's arm, swinging left and then dodging right around the man before kicking out one leg at his calf. The raja's soldier was too fast, sidestepping the blow before it could connect and then aiming a swift hook at Thaddeus's jaw. Apparently wanting to take them alive didn't mean they had to arrive at the raja's feet bruise-free. Thaddeus avoided the punch and then clasped both of his hands around the man's slicing fist, bending his knees and throwing his weight back onto the forest floor. The momentum took the attacker by surprise and he went sailing over Thaddeus's head, disappearing into the jungle undergrowth with a grunt and a rustle. Thaddeus was on his feet and running again in a second.

He could see Desai ahead of him, his own pursuer so close on the older man's heels that it could only be seconds before he was caught. Of Dita and J — or the two men who had chased after them — there was no sign, which at least gave Thaddeus the breathless hope that they were still free. Perhaps they had even reached the valley and found somewhere to hide there. Its lip leered at them from just a few hundred yards away, its dusty jagged edge tantalizingly close. Thaddeus kept running, not even turning to see whether the man he had downed had recovered himself as yet. As he ran he ducked to scoop a handful of the soft, dry forest dirt into his hand. Clutching it, he made straight for the man on Desai's tail, his lungs burning with the effort in the hot air of an Indian day.

He saw the soldier glance over his shoulder as he heard Thaddeus's footsteps. Thaddeus lunged forward, narrowly avoiding a tree root that reared up to snag his leg and then shoved the fistful of dirt into the man's face. He howled as the dust scratched against his eyes, immediately dropping back and doubling over with both hands to his face.

"Thank you, my young friend," Desai called over his shoulder breathlessly. "Keep going — we are almost there!"

"And then what?" he shouted back. "Will there be somewhere to hide?"

"You will see!"

The ground was sloping sharply upward. Thaddeus's legs burned with the renewed effort it took to climb the incline. There was a commotion ahead of them. Thaddeus brushed the sweat out of his eyes to see the two men who had followed Dita and J skittering back down the slope. One of them fell, rolling against a tree trunk before dragging himself up again. Thaddeus thought the two men would launch themselves toward them, but instead they simply seemed intent on getting back down the slope as fast as possible.

One of them passed him close enough for Thaddeus to see the look on the soldier's face.

It was full of terror.

Chapter 13

A NEW HEADING

The compass was set on a southeasterly heading, which took the airship back along the river they had been able to see from the plateau. It cut through the jungle like a pure blue line, its waters far clearer than any river Rémy had ever seen before. Through the airship's window she could see it twisting and turning through the trees as if it would never stop. Hours passed and the sun rose, and still all that Rémy could see below her were trees, punctuated by the rushing billow of that pure blue water. Several times she reached out to issue a sharp tap against the glass case of the compass, wondering whether perhaps it was broken. Or perhaps, she thought, since she didn't know what she was supposed to be looking for, she could have missed something below her on the ground. But then, surely, the compass would have done something — changed, somehow — to tell her so?

She had no one to ask, and so she and the airship flew on. Rémy wished that Thaddeus were there with her — or rather, that she was wherever he was, with him. It seemed terribly wrong to be leaving him to deal with whatever he would have to face alone. It was only Thaddeus's own words convincing her to go that kept her on her course. Otherwise she may have turned back, the puzzle box and its cryptic gift be damned.

As the day grew ever older, the landscape changed. Jungle gave way to open pasture that was dotted by only a few trees. Pasture gave way to more and more villages, all surrounded by neatly cultivated fields instead of unruly jungle. Then she saw towns and then, eventually, even a great walled city. Still there was no indication from the compass that Rémy had reached where it was taking her. It stayed resolutely on its southeasterly heading, not changing, not moving. As the shadows began to creep across the ground below her, Rémy grew impatient.

"Come on!" she exclaimed, picking up the compass

and looking at it closely as if it might suddenly tell her something new. "Is this a trick? Hmm? If Desai had not believed in you, I would have tossed you over the side of that plateau! Perhaps I should have anyway! Where are we going? Why aren't we there yet?"

The compass merely rocked slightly in her palm, its north and south hands shivering against her anger but the third hand holding firm to its course.

With a sigh, Rémy replaced the compass on the control panel and looked up to see a vast line of blue tinting her horizon. White flecks danced on its rolling peaks as it crashed toward her before breaking against the shore.

The airship had reached the ocean.

"Agh!" she cried, throwing her hands up in the air. "Now what? I am supposed to leave this place altogether? I am supposed to just fly out over the water? What?"

The compass refused to tell her anything different at all.

From the position of the burning bright sun and the shadows casting across the hot ground, Rémy thought it must be about four o'clock. Days were long here, and the sun would not set until at least eight. Four more hours to find whatever the compass was trying to show her.

Rémy sat down with a sigh and rubbed her hands over her face. "Well, I have come this far, yes?" she muttered to herself.

She flew on, planning to continue until sunset before turning back. If she kept on a reverse heading, she'd find her way back to the valley in time for tomorrow's first light. She'd be a day behind the others, but Rémy was fleet of foot, especially when the occasion called for it.

Rémy had given up hope that she'd actually find anything out here on the ocean. Below her the waves bobbed and splashed against each other, stretching on and on in what seemed to be an endless body of water. There were no islands on the horizon, no curves of land unexpectedly showing from the sea. There was nothing and no one.

"Well, old woman," Rémy muttered, leaning back in the chair and raising her shabby-booted feet to rest against the lip of the control panel. "You have played me for a fool, yes? I wonder where you are now, and how often you laugh at that lost little French girl who so wanted to believe you, eh?"

A sound pulled her attention back to the compass. It was moving — vibrating against the airship's control panel so hard that it skittered between the knobs and dials, bouncing slightly on the hammered metal surface. Rémy picked it up and saw that the third hand was folding back into itself, sliding back into the tiny slot it had appeared out of that morning. In another moment or so, it was impossible to tell that it had been there at all. The compass was just a compass once again, with two hands telling her which way was north and south, and nothing at all out of the ordinary besides.

Rémy's heart gave a slight judder and leaned over to look out of the window. This must be it. She must have reached her destination — the place the compass wanted her to find. But how could there be anything out here? Then, squinting into the glorious glare of the setting sun, she saw it.

Bobbing on the waves was a ship — three-masted, all of its sails proudly set out to catch the wind whipping across the churning waves that were burnished in amber as the sun sped toward sunset. Rémy flew toward it. Was this, finally, what the compass had wanted her to see?

As she neared, Rémy could see movement as the sailors realized what was coming toward them. Their shouts brought more men from below, until the deck was awash with them. None of them wore uniforms,

Rémy noted — instead, they were dressed in a vast array of styles that seemed to mix everything from coat tails to shabby cut-off trousers. It looked, Rémy thought, like an odd kind of circus, though what a circus would be doing out here on the ocean instead of performing in a town or city somewhere, she couldn't imagine.

Putting down the compass, she flew around the ship in an arc, leaning forward to see what was happening below. The people on deck were shouting at her in a rather unfriendly way. She saw two of them run for the main mast and begin to haul on a rope there, hoisting a flag up its length, their huge muscles straining with the effort.

The flag unfurled quickly, the wind catching its roll and whipping it out to stand proud against the prevailing wind.

It was dark — black, in fact, with a skull and cross-bones tattooed in white across it.

A Jolly Roger.

Rémy's stomach clenched sickly and she fumbled for the controls. Pirates! She had to get out of there. There was no telling what —

Something hit the hull with a sharp *thunk* and instantly the airship began to list to the side, pulling the nose around toward the pirates' bow. Rémy almost slid out of her chair as the airship juddered and she fought to pull her straight again, but without success. A moment later there was another *thunk* — this one hit toward the airship's tail, and suddenly Rémy felt herself being hauled in, pulled lower and lower toward the ship that bobbed below her on the waves.

In a panic, Rémy fought with the controls — the airship bucked and weaved like a goat caught in a rope, but to no avail. Another thunk followed, and then another, and with each came an extra tug that pulled the airship closer and closer to the pirates' boat.

She could hear them now, roaring as the airship got ever closer. Rémy had no idea what to do. The controls were all but useless, whirring hopelessly under her hands.

"Heave!" came a shout from outside, followed by a roar made up of many voices, *"Heave! Heave! Heave!"* Each jolt that brought Rémy lower was timed with a cry of *Heave!*, until the rhythm was as impossible to escape as the ship's inexorable journey downward.

Rémy leapt up from the controls — they were useless for now, anyway. She ran for the airship's ramp and the small axe that hung beside it. If she could sever the tethers that were drawing the airship in . . .

The sight that greeted her as the ramp came down was terrifying. The airship had been pulled so low that the hull was almost level with the pirate ship's deck. A dozen ropes with climbing spikes had been hurled toward her craft, embedding themselves into the hull as easily as a bare foot pressed into wet sand. Each rope was held in the grip of two pirates — they had looped the other ends of their ropes securely around their ship's guardrail and were now straining as they pulled the airship in, inch by inch. More stood by, screaming encouragement at their fellows. They were all terrifying to behold — scarred and tattooed, painted and bejeweled; they bared their teeth, screaming and shouting, caught up in a bloodlust meant purely for Rémy and the airship they were claiming as their prize.

Rémy edged as far out onto the ramp as she could, knowing she only had a matter of seconds. Raising the axe, she aimed for the farthest rope and swung, severing the thick cord in one heavy strike. The pirates who held the other end lost their balance as their weight suddenly had nothing to counter it. They sprawled backward, ending up on the deck in a pile that briefly filled the air with bellows of laughter instead of murder.

She swung for the next rope and did the same, scrambling backward as it flicked free, and then immediately swung for the next. The airship's nose twisted away as the tethers loosened their grip. For a moment Rémy felt a surge of hope — it was working! Then she felt a vibration shaking the ramp and turned. Over her shoulder she saw one of the pirates climbing nimbly toward her up the ropes that still tied the airship fast.

It was a woman. Her white teeth were bared in a terrifying grimace, the blade of a *talwar* clamped between them. Her hands, bedecked with spiked rings, gripped the twanging ropes as she surged toward Rémy, her blue eyes sparking fury. Rémy could see another long-bladed sword strapped to her back. In a second she was on the ramp, grabbing the sword from between her lips with one hand and grasping Rémy's shoulder with the other, hauling her back up the ramp and into the airship, knocking the axe from her hand.

The pirate woman dragged Rémy upright, her sword coming up to press viciously against Rémy's neck as she stared at her, seemingly transfixed by her face.

"Who are you?" the pirate demanded. "Who sent you?"

The airship juddered again and another pirate — a man this time — appeared in the open doorway.

"Bring her down," he said, dipping his head to fit his bulk into the small cabin. "He wants to —" The man broke off as he looked up and saw Rémy. Surprise burst across his face, creasing the ugly, jagged scar that bisected his left cheek from ear to mouth. A second later suspicion settled where the surprise had been a moment before. "He wants to see her."

"You," said the woman, hissing sharply into Rémy's ear, "are wanted below."

"What about the ship?" Rémy gasped, feeling the bite of the cold blade against her neck with every struggle. "I can't just leave it."

"It's secure," the man whom Rémy named to herself as Scar Face growled. "We will tow it behind us."

"But —"

There came another shout from outside, but this one was different. It was urgent, full of warning, and came from the bird's nest at the top of the main mast.

"Ship ahoy!" bellowed the voice. "Look lively, lads! They've got their cannon —"

There was the sound of a huge crash, like thunder rolling in the distance, followed by a low, swift whistle. The pirate holding Rémy swung around, looking out of the open ramp. Below them on deck, the pirates scattered, yelling, running for their posts as the whistle grew louder.

A second later a cannonball broadsided the pirate ship with a force that caused the entire vessel to buckle. It crashed through the second deck, sending wave after wave of splintered wood into the air, carried by the wind. Pandemonium reigned above — pirates wielding rifles and pistols, huge spiked metal balls on chains and all manner of swords. Then they let loose their own cannon, two at once — one from forward and one from aft, the recoil shaking the ship almost as badly as the strike had done a moment earlier. The airship slewed sideways, buffeted by the force as she strained against her tethers.

"Incoming!" bellowed the lookout in the bird's nest. Another rolling crash of cannon-thunder echoed over the melee. The sails of the pirate ship flapped and shuddered and as they dipped, another ship came into view, swung sideways and with all her cannon gates open.

"It's the British," cried one of the men. "They've found us. That infernal air-boat has led them to us!"

"Listen to me," Rémy cried. "If one of those cannon balls hits the airship, we will all burn — your ship and mine! It's not like your ship, it cannot take a single strike — it will explode!"

The female pirate shook Rémy like a rat. "You lie!"

"No! I don't! You have to —"

The second cannon caught the pirate ship a glancing blow forward, smashing into its nose. Flames licked along the guardrail and there were shouts for buckets and water.

"I swear," said Rémy, "I am not lying. Just one flame like that one and we're all done for."

The female pirate snarled with anger and released Rémy, flinging her away so that she crashed against the airship's control panel and stumbled against the chair. Just as she did so, another cannonball fired from the British frigate crashed into the ship below. Rémy couldn't see what was happening, but from the frantic cries of the people below she knew it must have been a hard hit.

"He's going to have to run for it," exclaimed Scar Face. "We're no match for their firepower, but the *Black Star* can outrun their bucket of bolts! We're not at anchor! Why isn't he *running*?"

As if someone below had heard him, a shout echoed up from below. "Cut it loose!" came the cry. "The air beastie is dragging us back. The British have got us like sitting ducks! Cut it loose!"

The woman pirate leaned out of the window. "We cannot lose this prize!"

"Take it to the cove at Maginapundi," came back the answering shout. "Do it now!"

With a curse, the woman raised her sword and slashed at the tangled ropes still holding the airship fast to the deck. With a jerk the airship was free. It rose away from the pirate ship, soaring into the air like a freed bird. Rémy leaned over the controls, yawing the craft around as she almost tangled with the pirate ship's sails. She swung the airship toward the coast as the female pirate and Scar Face dragged up the ramp and secured it shut.

A second later Rémy felt the bite of a blade at her neck once more.

"Now," hissed the woman into her ear. "I have had to abandon my ship for you, *anukarana*. So one wrong move and I will not hesitate to part your head from your shoulders. Understand?"

Chapter 14

INTO THE VALLEY

$\mathcal{T}$hey crested the stony ridge and fell into a different world.

Unexpectedly soft earth dropped away from him and Thaddeus stumbled, fetching up against the rough trunk of a tree that barred his descent. He crashed to his knees, feeling a stab of pain in his shoulder where the tree's harsh bark had scraped the skin. He shook his head as if to clear it — convinced for a moment that he had gone deaf. Ahead of him, farther down the slope that careened sharply into the valley's dim depths, he could see J helping Dita to her feet. Thaddeus heard the crackle of twigs as the two youngsters regained their footing, and realized after all that he hadn't lost his hearing. It was just that the valley had sucked them into the kind of ringing, noisy quiet that stuffed the ears as surely as scraps of rag. After the noisy chaos of their fight with the raja's men, the sudden cease of sound was doubly confusing and distinctly unsettling.

He got to his feet, looking around for Desai. The older man was gingerly making his way down through the trees toward him. Of the raja's soldiers there was no sign. It was as if they had disappeared into thin air.

"What happened?" Thaddeus asked. He spoke in a whisper but his words still sounded loud in the valley's cloying quiet. "The soldiers — where did they go?"

Desai paused, turning to glance back up the ridge. Then he looked at Thaddeus with a slight smile. "They are afraid to enter the valley. More afraid than they are of disobeying their master's orders."

Thaddeus looked around, feeling a deep prickle of unease move across his shoulder blades. "Why? Just because of the legend?"

"Yes. It is superstition, mainly."

He looked back at Desai with one eyebrow raised. "Mainly?"

Desai clapped him on the shoulder. "Courage, Thaddeus. I know you have such a quality or you would not be here at all. Come — night will fall early here, and we should cover as much ground as we can before then."

Thaddeus watched as his friend went ahead to Dita and J, who were looking as troubled as he felt. Then, quietly, slowly, they all began to move — Desai in front leading the way, Thaddeus making up the rear.

"Stay close," Desai counseled them all in a whisper that would have carried like a leaf on a breeze anywhere else, but here cracked like a dry twig, "and stay alert. We are in strange country now."

It was true. Even the foliage looked different. The trees squatted fatly over their heads with large leaves far thicker than the ones Thaddeus had grown used to seeing over the months of their journey through India. The greens were deeper, darker, tinged with purple and veined with faint silver lines that glittered in the gloomy afternoon light. The ground was thickly clogged with dead leaves that shifted under foot as Thaddeus walked, rippling as if he were walking across a serpent's patterned spine. But there was no life here, save for the trees. No creatures rustled in the dull branches as they passed beneath, no insects skittered from the wake of their footfall. Save for the strange leaves, the valley felt abandoned — and if so,

Thaddeus would not blame those who had chosen to flee. He wasn't so far off doing so himself, however courageous Desai thought him to be.

Still, Thaddeus thought to himself, *this awful quiet does give us one advantage — we'll hear any attackers coming a mile off.*

They walked on, deeper and deeper into the valley. The light here was mediocre — fading as if the sun was setting, although it could barely be later than four o'clock in the afternoon. Thaddeus looked up and saw above him a dense roof made from the overlapping leaves, so thick that it stopped almost all light from filtering to the ground.

Mist twisted through the trees, weaving around the trunks like snakes. The air grew colder, as if the heat of India herself had been siphoned from the valley.

"I don't like this," muttered J. He and Dita were walking with their hands clasped tightly in each other's, shoulders bumping as they huddled close together.

Dita said nothing, staring fearfully around her as the mist seeped toward the group, growing denser by the second.

"We must move faster," said Desai, his voice echoing to Thaddeus as if from a great distance, even though he was only a few feet away. "And try to stay out of the mist."

"How?" J protested. "The stuff is everywhere! It's like wading through cold molasses, an' —"

Dita emitted a sharp scream that made them all jump. She clutched J even closer, her thin fingers bunching into his shirt as she peered wildly through the mist.

"What?" Thaddeus exclaimed his heart pounding. "What did you see?"

"I — I don't know," Dita cried. "A — a face, I think. A face without eyes, only black holes where the eyes should be, and . . . and . . ." Her voice faded to a whisper and Thaddeus could see that she was shaking.

"And what?" he probed gently, trying to sound calm even though he felt as terrified as the girl looked. "What else, Dita?"

"Teeth," she whispered, so quietly he had to lean forward to hear her despite the silence around them. "Rows and rows of sharp white teeth."

"Come," said Desai, "we must keep walking. This mist — it pulls strange tricks on the mind. Do not believe everything you think you see."

"What should we believe then, eh?" cried J as Desai waved them on. "If we can't believe our own eyes, like, then what should we believe?"

"We'll be fine, J," said Thaddeus, trying to tell himself that it was true. "We'll stick together and keep moving, all right? Everything will be fine."

They followed Desai, but Dita was still shaking like a leaf. With every snap of a twig beneath their feet or fresh billow of mist reaching out at them as bony fingers would, she flinched, her thin face pale.

"We 'ave to go back," said J, "Whatever's down 'ere, we ain't ready for it. There ain't enough of us, fer a start!"

Dita raised her head from his shoulder. "No," she said firmly. "We must go on, *ja*? We must."

"But you —"

"You stay close to me," she said. "You stay close to me and I will be — how do you say it? Right as rain, dirty boy. *Right as rain.*"

J hugged her and they stumbled on, although by now the mist was so thick that it was hard to see more than a foot or two in front of them. Thaddeus stumbled over a gnarled tree root protruding like a broken limb from the leaves under foot. In the second that it took him to right himself, he'd fallen behind enough to lose the others. A spark of panic burst through his heart.

"Desai!" he shouted. "J, Dita! Wait!"

The mist rushed in around him, sheets of thick gray coldness as palpable and heavy as blankets left out in the rain. Thaddeus batted it away from his face and arms, shouting for his friends again, trying to stem the panic as the mist touched his face and slid along his hair.

Ahead of him he heard noises — another piercing scream from Dita, shouting from J and, he thought, even from Desai, too. Thaddeus stumbled forward, trying to head for the sounds — it felt as if he were forcing his way through a heavy curtain as he battled against the mist. He could hear other noises now, too — a strange, low chanting, rising around him like another wave of fog. It was impossible to make out the words — if they even *were* words — but they rolled closer before snapping away sharply, as if whoever was speaking them was darting in close to his ear and darting away again before Thaddeus had a chance to turn and see them.

Then, as quickly as it had enveloped him, the mist rolled back. It was as if someone had opened a window and pulled it out. As he watched, it drew back in columns that looked disturbingly like tentacles — coiling, curling, sinuous, it crept back between the trees to wherever it had come from.

Thaddeus found himself out of breath, as if he'd been running. He spun around, looking for his companions. They emerged from the mist like statues — Desai, J . . . but no Dita. He looked around wildly, searching the forest as it came into view.

"Dita!" J shouted, frantic. "Where are you?"

There was no answer. The forest was as silent as it had been when they first rushed over the ridge. Thaddeus went to J and grabbed his arm.

"What happened?" he asked, but the boy shook his head miserably.

"I don't know! She were here one minute — holding on to me, like, and then . . . and then . . . she were gone. She told me, Thaddeus, didn't she? She told me to stay close, and she'd be fine. But she wasn't fine — she wasn't . . ."

Thaddeus hugged him. "We'll find her, J. Don't worry. We'll get Dita back, and she'll be just fine."

Desai moved to Thaddeus's shoulder, although he was looking out into the darkness, which seemed even deeper than before.

"We must go," he said. "The power of the Sapphire Cutlass has already grown stronger than I realized. They will not stop until they have us all, and if we want to save Dita then we must stay free."

J sniffed and wiped the back of his hand under his nose. "All right. Which way is it then? I'm all turned about after the mist, like."

Desai paused for a moment, looking around. Then he gestured. "It is this way."

"You sure?" J asked defiantly. "Because it all looks the same to me and I don't want to end up wasting time going in the wrong direction, right?"

Desai looked at the boy steadily. "J. Trust me. I know where we're going."

J stared back again for another moment. "All right then. Let's get on wiv it." He turned and stomped off.

"J," said Thaddeus, catching up with him and laying a hand on his shoulder. "Calm down."

J shrugged him off, his face a picture of anger. "I said we shoulda turned back. Didn't I? Didn't I say so, Mr. Rec?"

"Yes, J, you did. And Dita said no, didn't she? She wanted to carry on, because she knows how important this is. So that's what we're going to do. We'll carry on, we'll get her back, we'll get out of here, and we'll do it together. All right?"

J didn't have a chance to answer. There came a warning shout from Desai, and Thaddeus turned to see the mist rushing in again. It came faster this time, a gray wall that swallowed them up almost before they'd even seen it coming. He reached for J, standing right next to him, and felt the boy being pulled away even before he heard him yell.

Thaddeus heard Desai shout, too, and then a commotion that could only mean the older man was fighting an attacker. Thaddeus felt solid shapes moving around him, had the fleeting impression of faces in the mist, darting in and darting away again. The chanting returned — louder this time, he thought, but it could also just have been that it was closer.

Desai's shouts stopped as suddenly as they started, leaving only the dull roar of the chant, roving closer and closer. Thaddeus spun around, listening for any sign that his friends were still nearby, but heard nothing.

He felt something slide down his arm — fingers. Thaddeus jerked himself away, backing into the mist, but doing so bumped him into something else — something grasping, pulling at his shirt, drawing him in. He pulled away again, spinning to face his attacker, but there was nothing but the infernal gray blankness and the endless, endless chanting.

A feeling of hopelessness washed over him as he saw ghostly faces peering out of the mist. The others were gone, he knew that — their silence was as loud as the chant that droned on and on like some kind of drug. He would be taken, too, and who only knew where — somewhere none of them would ever be found, much less where they could hope to stop whatever the Sapphire Cutlass had planned beyond this valley of terrors.

The chanting stopped. Thaddeus knew he was out of time.

As one, the figures lunged toward him. Cruel hands reached for him, grasping his arms, his legs, tightening around his neck.

{Chapter 15}

ANUKARANA

The waves lapped at the dark shoreline. Rémy shivered in the breeze that whisked across the pale sand. Now that the sun had set — had been set, in fact, for an hour or so — the air had chilled again. In fact, it was becoming so cold that the two pirates holding her captive were in the process of building a large fire. Flames licked at the dry wood they had collected from the shore, the orange flickers growing by the second, their crackle and fizz filling the restless salt air.

Rémy sat on the sand with her back against a rock, her hands and feet tied so that she could not move even to rub her cold arms. The fire had been constructed in the sheltered shadow of a spit of stone that jutted out from the even taller cliffs around them. It would be invisible to anyone looking toward the shore from the ocean, and indeed to anyone looking from inland, too, unless they happened to lean directly over the crumbling cliff edge and look down. It was a good spot to hide — one that her captors were obviously very familiar with, judging from the remains of old fires dotted about the shore.

The airship stood behind them where Rémy had been forced to land it, a safe distance from the growing fire. The balloon was almost completely deflated — the ruby exhausted from its long two days of flight.

Rémy rolled her shoulders, hating being so help-less. As she watched, the female pirate moved slowly in Rémy's direction, her attention on the fire as she rubbed her hands together. Rémy watched her profile with interest. She didn't think this girl was much older than she was. Her face was built of sharp and elegant angles — a proud forehead, a pointed nose pierced with a tiny diamond that glinted like a star against her skin. Her eyes were large and clear, even in the darkness. The girl's long black hair swept back from her face in a thick, unfussy plait that fell almost to her waist. There were scars, too — almost as many as Rémy had noticed on the men — slashes that patterned her arms and neck, a testament to a hard life. The girl's clothes were shabby and functional — a cropped green top without sleeves, baggy brown trousers bound with a belt at the waist and what looked like strips of leather at the calves, where they were pushed into scuffed tan boots that laced almost to the knee. The *talwar* hung in a leather scabbard from her belt, her hand hovering near its hilt as if ready to draw it at a moment's notice.

"How long have you been a pirate?" Rémy asked quietly.

The girl started as if she'd forgotten Rémy was even there, looking at her for a second before setting her mouth in a line and looking away.

"I used to be part of a circus," Rémy went on, trying to find something that they might have in common. "My master made me steal almost as soon as I could walk. It's not a great life, is it?"

The girl turned and looked at her again, her eyes piercing and disdainful in the firelight. "Speak for yourself, *anukarana*," she said in a low voice. "I have a very good life. I am my own master."

"You called me that before," said Rémy. "*Anu* . . . *Anukarana?*"

The girl stared hard at the fire, her eyes glittering in the flickering light. "Yes."

"What does it mean?"

The girl was silent for a moment, her shoulders hunched against her knees. Then she looked at Rémy, her face expressionless. "In my language it means 'imitator.'"

"Why do you call me that?"

She turned back to the fire. "You know."

"I don't," said Rémy. "I promise you, I don't. Please tell me."

The girl didn't look at her again, or speak another word, as if the fire was telling her secrets that she had to strain to hear.

"I can't explain how I found your ship," Rémy said quietly. "I don't think you would believe me if I told you. But I had a reason — a good one. I was looking for my brother. My twin."

Rémy saw the girl's shoulders tense and knew that she'd heard what Rémy had said.

"Is there someone aboard your ship who looks like me?" Rémy asked. "Is that why you called me an imitator? Is that why you all look at me," she indicated Scar Face, sitting on the other side of the fire, "as if you have seen me before?"

The girl turned to look at her again. "Who sent you?" she asked. "Your ship bears the Union Jack.

Have the British paid to put a curse upon Kai's soul? Is that why you are here, *anukarana*? To trick us into betraying him because they can find no other way to catch him?"

"Kai?" Rémy asked, her heart speeding up. "Who is that? Does he — does he look like me?"

The girl smiled, though the gesture was far from friendly. "If you truly do not know, you will find out soon enough. When he comes with the others."

"Do you mean your ship?" Rémy asked. "How do you know they'll make it? They took heavy damage. What if they were destroyed?"

The girl put back her head and laughed. "Impossible, *anukarana*. Kai leads a charmed life. He will survive, no matter what you or his other enemies throw at him."

"I'm not — I'm *not* his enemy," Rémy said, frustrated, then stopped as a thought occurred to her. "He — Kai — you say he has a charmed life. Does he have a talisman? Perhaps a precious stone — an opal, maybe — that he wears around his neck?"

The girl looked at her sharply, eyes narrowed and fingers flexed. She relaxed a little and looked back to the fire. "I am Upala," she said softly. "I am his opal, and his talisman. I will always keep him safe."

Rémy was about to ask her what she meant when a

mighty yell echoed against the cliff walls and reverberated around the beach. At first Rémy thought it was
the wind playing tricks, but then it came again, closer
this time. She twisted around, looking toward the
water as Upala stood.

The pirate's vessel crested the waves as it rounded
the cliff to enter the cove. It was battered and scarred,
but it was whole — and on its deck stood every one of
Upala's shipmates, apparently unharmed.

The ship dropped anchor and the pirates began to
jump over the side, splashing into the shallows and
wading through the water like a tide of their own
making. They were singing and dancing, swaggering
as they drew nearer, evidently pleased with themselves.

The pirates rushed up the beach toward the fire,
scattering sand into the breeze around them. All
around her, they moved in flurries of color and sound.
It felt unreal to Rémy as she watched everything from
very far away, atop one of the cliffs that served as their
shelter. Gone were the terrifying cries that had greeted
the airship, replaced now by laughter and wild yells of
celebration.

For a second, the mass of bodies parted, like two
tides drawing away from each other. Rémy looked
through the gap and saw a pirate striding up the sand

against the wind. He was thin and wiry, dressed all in black — black boots, tied up to his calves, black breeches, black shirt. On his head was a black tri-corn hat.

Rémy felt her heart judder as he turned, knowing what she was about to see even before she had actually seen it. And suddenly, there he was. It was like looking in a mirror where everything is recognizable although very slightly skewed. This man, this pirate dressed in black — he looked like her. He looked like Rémy.

He didn't look in her direction at all. She watched him stride across the sand, weaving around his carousing shipmates with complete determination. Rémy realized that he was making for Upala. A smile burst across her face as she saw him — the first genuine one Rémy had seen her give in all the hours they had spent together that day. The two pirates walked toward each other and Rémy expected them to embrace, but instead they stopped a pace or so in front of each other, seeming suddenly awkward. Upala dipped her head, nodded, and then shrugged at something he said. Then she looked in Rémy's direction, said something, and pointed.

The man turned. He looked straight at Rémy

with a look sharp enough to pierce stone. Her heart began to thump as he strode toward her, no trace of surprise on his scarred face. The pirate walked until he stood a hair's breadth away, his face a mirror that Rémy could easily have pressed her nose to.

"Well, well," he whispered. "So here you are at last, Rémy Brunel."

Rémy opened her mouth, but found it impossible to get any sound past the lump that had unexpectedly formed in her throat. In any case, what was she to say? It seemed that this pirate knew her, and of course she should know him, but she did not.

The face before her — so familiar and yet so completely unknown — studied her carefully. The pirate's eyes narrowed slightly.

"My name is Kai," he said softly. "Do you not even know that, little sister?"

{*Chapter 16*}

THE REUNION

*T*he pirates' celebratory mood continued long into the night. The fire burned brightly, and they danced on the sand in the light of the flames as they roasted fish freshly caught from the ocean for their supper. Rémy sat on the sand beside the pirate captain — her brother, and not only her brother, her true twin. Together they looked out at the shenanigans before them.

Upala had left them to talk and was now dancing with one of the largest men Rémy had ever seen, even accounting for all her years of traveling with the circus. Rémy glanced at Kai and saw that her brother's gaze was fixed on the fierce female pirate. Upala had removed her boots and was dancing barefoot with such carefree abandon that it was easy to forget just how fearsome she could look with a sword in her hand and a scowl on her face. Kai watched her with an expression that softened the hardest lines of his face, too, and seeing this Rémy looked away, a slight pang piercing her heart. Kai's regard for Upala was obvious, and it made her think of Thaddeus. She wondered how he and the others were, and wished she were with them. The sooner she could follow their trail, the better. Which meant she shouldn't merely be sitting here, watching this celebration.

"You did not seem surprised to see me," she began, leaning closer to Kai so that her voice carried over the noise of the party.

Kai offered a slight smile, but his gaze remained fixed on the festivities. "Oh, I was surprised — to see you *here*, anyway."

"I never even knew I had a brother," Rémy told him. "Not until a few months ago. But you knew you had a sister, all along?"

The pirate turned to look at her at last, a dark light in his eyes. "I knew about the curse that hangs over our family. I knew what part the raja and that rat Gustave had in it and I knew, yes, I knew, that I was a twin. But life is difficult enough, Rémy, without dwelling on those things you cannot change. If you are waiting for me to apologize for not searching for you, you will wait a long time. I have had hard enough work just keeping myself alive."

Rémy looked away, pained. "That's not what I meant," she said, blinking hard as she stared at the flames. "I just do not understand why you knew when I did not."

Kai leaned forward to pick up a piece of driftwood at his feet and turned it in his hands. "When our parents separated, they each took one of us. Our mother took you. Our father took me."

"And brought you back here? To India?"

Her twin shrugged. "He died before I was old enough to think to ask him why. Maybe he thought he could find a way to lift the curse himself. He always talked of you — you and our mother. He loved you both. They just . . . could not be together, all the time that the curse was in place. And he never found a way to break it."

"It is broken now," Rémy told him. "You know that, don't you?"

Kai stopped twirling the stick, but he didn't look up. His face took on a frown. "What do you mean?"

"I have a friend. His name is Desai. He is from here,

but he has spent many years living in London. The diamond that our parents stole from the raja all those years ago — I found it, Kai. Desai brought it back here, to lift the curse. We are both free."

Kai slowly lifted his head and looked out at the dancers again. The tune had changed, but the music was still just as fast. Upala weaved in and out of the other dancers, laughing as she twisted and turned, her bare feet scattering flurries of sand into the air. Kai's eyes found her in the crowd, as Rémy suspected they always would. "The curse . . . is *broken?*" he repeated slowly.

"Yes, thanks to Desai."

"He must be a great friend, indeed."

Rémy saw her chance and seized it. "He is. He is a great friend and a great man. At this moment he is trying to save this place from a terrible danger."

Her brother turned to look at her. "A danger? What danger?"

Rémy took a deep breath. "It is called the Sapphire Cutlass. Have you heard of it?"

Kai stared at her for a moment, then gave a bitter laugh. "Your friend has been telling you fairy stories, little sister. There are far worse dangers here than a fable like the Sapphire Cutlass. Monsters that you, in your soft little circus life, could not possibly imagine."

Rémy prickled at that. "Dangers such as running into a band of marauding pirates, for example?"

Kai shook his head. "We are not the people to fear here — not for good, ordinary folk, in any case. We do what we do to help the people of this country, not to hurt them. The British take everything from these people and give nothing back. They take their land, their crops, their jewels, their sons. What can be more monstrous than that? So the people turn to the person they think can help them — the raja, who is even worse. He forces them to fight against all his enemies in an army that has no firepower, no training — no hope of winning at all."

Rémy thought of the villages that the airship had stopped in before the jeweled man had attacked them — how in many of them there had only been the very young and the very old and the very sick. Suddenly it seemed obvious where the able-bodied had gone, and why the crops had gone untended.

"We take from both sides, and we do what we can to help with what we steal," Kai went on. "So you see, little sister, we have plenty of monsters already without borrowing them from children's stories."

"What if it isn't a children's story?" she pressed.

Kai laughed scornfully. "A woman made of sapphire with the power to tear whole armies asunder with her bare hands? How could it be anything but?"

Rémy shrugged. "Some people believe, yes? There is a cult, so Desai told me."

Kai threw the chunk of driftwood away. "So there is, he is right. A cult made of superstitious old men and women with nothing else to do with their time and nothing better to put their faith in."

"Desai says it is more than that. The cult has been growing, becoming more and more powerful," she said, thinking it better to leave out, at least for the moment, her friend's belief in the supernatural powers of the mountain and its sapphires. "He thinks someone is using the myth of the Sapphire Cutlass as a way to recruit more people."

Her brother looked at her thoughtfully. "Does he now? And what would be the good of that?"

Rémy shrugged. "People will do anything for something they believe in, isn't that right? Terrible things. Bad things. Desai thinks they are preparing for war."

"A war? Who with?"

"He doesn't know, but he thinks it is the raja's mystic, Sahoj, behind it. And if that's the case and the British find out, there will be a war for sure."

Kai raised his hands. "Well then, I say let them fight. If they wipe each other out, so much the better, eh?"

Rémy put her hand on his arm, leaning closer. "Really? You would want that? You would let those people you care so much for be caught in the middle of such a war?"

Her brother set his jaw and did not answer, staring at the fire with dark eyes.

"I have seen things, Kai. The airship I brought here — it is nothing compared to the machines of war that I know are out there. Metal soldiers with no feeling and no heart that can march for days without food and will fight without mercy; ships that can sail beneath the water so that no one will see them coming — powered by the earth itself and by gem stones like the one that our parents stole, all those years ago. You don't have to believe me — I can show you the ruby that makes my ship fly. I have seen things you wouldn't believe, brother, and they have all lead us here, to this place — to the Sapphire Cutlass. Perhaps the story is just a story, but whatever is happening in the name of that story should terrify us all."

"And say I were to believe your words, little sister? Say I were to feel as afraid as you — what would you have me do about it?"

"Help us. The people I traveled here with — good people, four of them — they are journeying into the valley of the Sapphire Cutlass as we speak. Come with me. You and your pirates. Come with me to find them — to help them, with whatever they find."

Kai turned to look at her. "Four people?" he said incredulously. "This man Desai believes you must fight an army — and he brought only three people with him?"

Rémy looked down at her feet. "He didn't bring us. He was imprisoned by the raja. We came looking for him and freed him."

"So . . . these people you brought with you," Kai said. "They are soldiers? Fighters of the first order? Fearsome warriors, able to fell armies as easily as the girl in the story. Yes?"

Rémy shifted uncomfortably. "Not exactly."

"Oh?" She could feel Kai watching her with sharp eyes. "Tell me, then. Who are they, these people who will defeat a supernatural army?"

Rémy shut her eyes. "One is a policeman. His name is Thaddeus Rec, from London. He is a brave and honorable man who will stop at nothing to do the right thing."

"A policeman," Kai repeated, his voice flat. "Well, I

hope you are starting at the bottom and working your way up, Rémy Brunel."

"Then there is J," Rémy went on, her heart sinking at her brother's unimpressed tone, but carrying on regardless. "He is swift and brave — I met him in London, too. He was a pickpocket then, but —"

"A pickpocket?" Kai interrupted her, his disbelief growing further. "This man Desai must be a fool. Who else but a fool would bring other fools with him to a battle?"

"J built the airship," Rémy said. "He built it from nothing but a book of words and scraps he found around Limehouse."

That shut her brother up. His eyebrows rose in surprise, and he looked over her head toward the craft sitting silently on the shore.

"Appearances can be deceptive," Rémy told him, "and I would have thought that a pirate, of all people, would know that."

Kai looked at her and grinned, his teeth straight and white apart from a single, black gap where he had lost one. The absence made him look fierce and reckless, and she longed to hear of the life her brother had led. Maybe they would have time, someday, to swap stories — of her life on the road, of his on the ocean.

But not now. She could tell that despite his interest, Kai was far from convinced by her story. She decided not to let on that two of Desai's party were children. Let him find out for himself if he agreed to help. And if he didn't — well, there would be no need for him to know in any case.

"And the final member of your little fighting force?" Kai prompted, as if he could read her thoughts. She wondered briefly if he could, but his question seemed genuine enough.

"Dita," Rémy said, scuffing her toes in the sand. "Small, wiry, and quick. She speaks many languages, has a head for heights, and is as brave as they come."

Kai looked out at the dancing pirates, once again finding Upala in the crowd. "Could she have a hope of bettering Upala in a fight?"

Rémy smiled privately at the thought of little Dita, who would barely reach Upala's waist, clashing blades with the female pirate. And yet . . . "She would do her best," Rémy told him truthfully, "and she would fight with her whole heart."

Kai nodded. "As Upala does," he said. "As it should be." Her brother sighed. "I admire you and your friends, little sister. It takes courage and spirit to go up against something with so few hands, especially with so little knowledge of what you may encounter."

"Then help us," Rémy urged. "If you truly live your life to help others, help us — and in doing so, help all of India. All of the world, perhaps. Help us before it is too late."

Kai shook his head. "Even if I thought it would make a difference — my people are fighters on water, not on land. On the ocean I can keep them safe, but on land they will be easy prey before we even reach the valley you speak of. Every one of them has a bounty on his head, put there by the British, who will kill them if they are caught. I will not lead them to certain death on the basis of a story," he said, holding up a hand before she could interrupt, "and a story is all you have, Rémy. Can't you see that?"

Rémy was silent for a few minutes. Then she said, "What if I gave you the airship?"

Kai looked surprised. "What?"

"Help us, and afterward, I will give you the airship. That would give you an advantage over the British, would it not?"

The pirate threw back his head and laughed. "Oh, little sister — look around you. If I wanted your ship, I could take it from you in a flat second."

"But you wouldn't know how to fly it," Rémy countered. "Help us, Kai, and when it's over I'll give you the airship — and I will teach you how to use it, too. You have my word."

Kai looked at her as if he were sizing up the truth of her statement. "And what about this J, who built it? Won't he be rather upset that you've given away his contraption?"

"Desai sent me to find you, Kai. I see that now. He knows we need your help. J will understand if it is the only way to secure it."

Kai looked over to the airship, rubbing his chin thoughtfully. He stood up, and Rémy followed as he crossed to where it waited patiently in the sand. Her brother ran his hands over the wood of the hull, and she could tell he was interested. What pirate wouldn't be? To be able to attack from the air — it would make Kai the undisputed king of the ocean.

Rémy heard a noise behind her and turned to see Upala approaching, her dark cheeks flushed pink from dancing. She stopped beside Rémy and put her hands on her hips, watching Kai as she caught her breath.

"What are you thinking?" she asked him over the noise of the party continuing behind them.

"That this would give us the advantage we so desperately need," Kai said as he continued to contemplate the airship.

Upala nodded, crossing her arms. "Then it's fortunate we have the *anukarana* to teach us how to use it."

"I'll teach you, if you help me," Rémy said firmly.

"Help you do what?" Upala asked, looking between the twins suspiciously.

Kai turned and walked back toward them. "Upala. You and the rest of the crew take the ship back to our safe harbor. I'll join you there — with the airship — when I can."

"Why?" Upala asked. "Where are you going?"

"To see whether what my sister has told me about the Sapphire Cutlass is true."

"I believe it is," said Rémy, "and if it is we need more help than just you, Kai."

"Well, I am all you're getting, little sister. I'll not drag anyone else along for what could be a one-way trip."

"You're going with her?" Upala looked appalled. "It could be a trap!"

"Yes," agreed Kai, watching Rémy steadily, "it could be. But somehow I don't think so. Or if it is, it's not one set by her. So I will go with her and find out."

Rémy held her brother's gaze, feeling her heart flood with relief. It wasn't what Desai had been hoping for, she was sure of that — one extra pair of hands against whatever they would have to face. But it was better than nothing — and if they could be on their way immediately, then so much the better.

By now the rest of the pirates had realized that something was afoot. The music and dancing had stopped, and Kai's crew had formed a semi-circle around them, quietly watching what was going on.

"I'm coming with you," Upala declared. "I will not let you go alone."

"It'll be safer if you —"

"Safer!" Upala scoffed, cutting him off. "What do I care about staying safe?"

"I care," Kai told her, the quiet, clipped words seeming to kill all other noise around them save for the crackle of the fire. The two pirates stared at each other, and Rémy realized that something significant had happened in that one, small moment. She had assumed they were a couple, but perhaps she was wrong. She remembered, then, her brother's reaction when he'd learned they were no longer cursed. Had he been holding back? Had he kept his distance from Upala because he knew about the curse?

"I am coming with you, Kai," Upala said into the quiet. "If you don't let me travel with you I will follow on foot. Do you understand?"

"If we are going to go at all," Rémy said into another silence, "then we should go now."

Chapter 17

INSIDE THE MOUNTAIN

He was on a trapeze, and he didn't like it.

Thaddeus could feel himself swinging in midair — back and forth, back and forth — but around him was only darkness. He couldn't see the ground, or even the contraption that was holding him up. He felt queasy and wrong, but he didn't know how to stop the swinging. Back and forth, back and forth . . .

Thaddeus!

A voice soared to him out of the darkness. He had heard it before, he realized as he heard it again, but it was farther away this time. Or perhaps he was the one who had been farther away — perhaps they were both on a trapeze.

Thaddeus!

Who did he know who would be comfortable on a trapeze?

Thaddeus!

Rémy Brunel! It could only be her up here, swinging with him in the darkness. Wherever "here" was — at the moment he couldn't tell, because everything was so dark, and the trapeze just would not stop moving . . . He tried to twist around and see what was behind him, but in doing so, he almost slipped from the swing completely. He flailed with his arms, clutching at anything he could. His hands found cold, hard rungs and he held on.

"Thaddeus!"

The voice shouting at him suddenly got much louder. Thaddeus frowned. It wasn't Rémy after all. It was —

"Mr. Rec! Would you please just bleedin' well WAKE UP!"

J!

Thaddeus jerked awake and immediately wished he hadn't. Pain smashed into his temple as if someone had cracked it hard with a rock. He clutched his head, wondering for a split second if he'd been in The Grapes the previous night, before remembering that he hadn't been at the Limehouse drinking spot for months.

"Thaddeus!"

"All right, all right," he mumbled back. "I'm awake, I'm —"

He turned around, slipped, and fell. He cried out before something abruptly broke his fall a second later, or rather, two somethings that were part of a larger something all together. Thaddeus blinked, trying to clear his head enough to focus. He could feel his legs dangling into thin air, and there was that infernal swinging again — back and forth, back and forth — through chilled air.

Even with his eyes open, it was dark, although not quite as dark as it had been in his dream. There was a faint light coming from somewhere — yellow, like a burning torch. It gave enough of a glow to show him where he had fetched up.

Thaddeus Rec was in a cage.

"What the —"

"Are you all right?" he heard Dita's voice call from behind him. Thaddeus turned his head and saw that she was in a cage, too, hanging beside him, her small hands clutching at the golden bars that imprisoned her as she stared anxiously at him.

"Thaddeus? Are you hurt?" That was Desai, on the other side of him, in another cage, peering through the dim light and the obstruction of yet another barred prison, this one holding J.

Thaddeus looked down at himself, still dazed from the pain of whatever blow his head had encountered. His legs had fallen between two of the rungs of his prison and he was dangling out of the bottom of it — their cages were suspended, apparently hanging above the ground, which he could not see through the darkness.

He struggled, pulling himself up and balancing his feet on two of the rungs — crouching, as the others were. It wasn't comfortable, but then presumably whoever had built the cages hadn't been very concerned about the comfort of their prisoners. They hung there in a line: Desai, then Dita, then J, then Thaddeus, in four cages each just large enough to hold a grown man, cubes made of golden bars not quite far enough apart for agile little Dita to squeeze between them. Thaddeus looked up to see that the roof of his cage bore a hatch, and beside the hatch was a sturdy ring through which had been threaded a hook, and from this hook led a chain as thick as Thaddeus's arm. It led up to a large metal track set in the roof of the cavern that stretched away into the gloom around them. It instantly reminded Thaddeus of what they had found in the Comte de Cantal's mountain catacombs.

"Where — where are we?" he managed, his voice rasping. His mouth felt as dry and dusty as the floorboards of the Professor's workshop.

"Where'd you fink?" J asked. "Looks like it didn't turn out to be as 'ard to get into the ruddy mountain as Mr. Desai fought it were going to be, eh?"

Thaddeus put a hand to his head as he looked up again. The throbbing was diminishing a little, but he'd have given his best trousers for a cool glass of water.

"Are the rest of you all right?" he asked. "None of you are hurt?"

"It looks as if you got the worst of it, my boy," said Desai.

Thaddeus looked around again, trying to see where they were. Their voices echoed as they spoke, he noticed. Wherever it was that they had ended up, it was large.

"Have you shouted for anyone?"

"Other than you, you mean?" J asked. "Yeah, we've shouted. Nuffin' doin'. No one's come to see us at all since they stuck us in 'ere. But I suppose they don't need to, do they? Seeing as there's no way any of us can get out."

Thaddeus looked up at the roof of the cage again.

"Makes you wish Rémy were here, don't it?" J added. "She'd be up there picking that lock in no time. As it is, none of the rest of us can manage it."

"I have tried," Dita said softly. "I'll keep trying, but I'm just not as good as Rémy is."

"Don't you worry, Miss," J soothed. "It ain't your fault. No one is, are they?"

Thaddeus looked over at Desai, whose face he could only just make out in the darkness pressing in on them. "Any ideas, Desai?" he asked. "You haven't got . . . I don't know, anything hidden in those robes of yours that might get us out of here?" Several times in the past Desai had surprised them all by producing potions capable of amazing feats — the ability to melt metal being one of them.

Desai shook his head. "My apologies, Thaddeus. After so many weeks in captivity at the Raja's behest, I am afraid my supplies have been well and truly plundered."

Thaddeus nodded slowly, and then wished he hadn't. He shut his eyes briefly, trying to close out the pain, but doing so just made him more aware of the gentle swing of the cage. J was right — Rémy would be in her element here. Little Bird, the girl who could fly without wings, and whom no cage had yet managed to enclose — at least, not for long.

"All right," he said. "Well, let's look at this rationally and see what we can come up with. It's reasonable to assume that we're still inside the valley, isn't it? And we've most likely been taken by the Sapphire Cutlass. Which means we're probably inside the mountain — in the mines themselves. Yes?"

"I would say that is a reasonable deduction," agreed Desai.

"Fat lot of good that does us," J muttered loudly.

"J," Thaddeus sighed. "Look, I know you're angry, but —"

"Damn right I'm angry!" J burst out, his knuckles white where his hands gripped the rungs. "I told yer — didn't I? I said we should turn back, and now look where we've ended up! You can be rational all you like, Mr. Rec, but we ain't getting ourselves out of 'ere in a hurry, are we? We're stuck, and gawd only knows what the people who put us in 'ere 'ave got planned fer us!"

"J," cried Dita, "don't say that!"

J looked past Thaddeus to the girl, his face softening. "Sorry," he said. "Sorry. We'll be all right. Course we will. It's just . . ."

A noise swelled below them, quiet at first, but growing. Thaddeus felt the hairs rise on the back of his neck as he realized what it was. It was voices, chanting — the same chant that had surrounded them out on the fogged valley floor was rising to them again from somewhere below their cages, a collective murmur growing louder and louder, the sound of too many voices to count united in one repeated mantra.

"Where the bleedin' 'eck 'ave they come from?" J cried. "'Ave they been down there all along, just being really quiet, like?"

For some reason, the thought made Thaddeus shiver. Then, somewhere off to his distant right, there came a noise like the sound of a giant match being struck: a harsh rasp, a fizz as a new flame added more light to the darkness. They all scrambled to the other side of their cages, stepping clumsily from one rung to another, careful not to slip into the spaces between as the motion jerked and shuddered their dangling prisons.

A large wooden torch had been lit. It burned brightly in the darkness, illuminating a yellow circle around itself. It had been pinned to hewn gray stone above a narrow walkway cut from more of the same rock. Another torch was lit farther along the wall, then another and another, tracing a route that circled where Thaddeus and his friends hung in their cages.

"If we ever get out of here," came J's plaintive voice as their surroundings slowly came into view, "I ain't never going anywhere near a mountain again. You hear me? Not a mountain, not a cave, not an underground bleedin' tunnel. Never again. I's seen enough of 'em to last me five lifetimes!"

They were in a large cavern. J was right — it could have been Lord Abernathy's submarine base beneath London, or the one housing the Comte de Cantal's metal army in France. It made sense, Thaddeus supposed. If one were drawn to nefarious deeds, it was natural to find somewhere such as this to hide them. Although, he reflected for a moment, there was nothing natural about any of the things they had found in such places. He felt exactly as J did — that if they made it out of this particular predicament, he had had enough of dark places to last him a lifetime. Give him sun, blue sky, and a beach that stretched for as far as the eye could see . . .

If they got out of here. Which, as he looked around, Thaddeus realized would be nigh-on impossible.

The cavern was a rough oval shape, so large that even with the torches burning their brightest, there were parts of it that were still in darkness. Into its walls had been hewn huge, curved alcoves — eight in total, Thaddeus counted — and in each alcove stood a massive, intricately carved statue. Each one of the huge stone figures depicted the same woman, her face contorted into a terrifying grimace of abject rage. Her fingers bore talons instead of nails, and around her feet wove stone snakes. The carving was so detailed that despite her inhuman size, Thaddeus could almost believe that at any moment, the carved woman would step out of her resting place.

The cages in which Thaddeus and the others were trapped hung from a large iron hook in the ceiling, giving him a good view of the whole place. Thaddeus looked around carefully, fixing it in his mind as he searched for a way out. The cavern was on four levels. Below them was a pit, its depths hidden from view by shadows. This pit had been carved beside a raised stone stage that formed one end of the cavern. A narrow channel had been sunk into the raised rock, leading from near the front of the stage and disappearing back through an archway in the cavern wall at its rear. Opposite where the prisoners swung, at the far side of the stage, a wide, sloping stone path lead up to another archway that stood between two of the massive statues.

Squinting through the flickering gloom, Thaddeus realized that the chains from which their cages dangled fed through the hoop above them and ran across the cavern's ceiling to a winch beside this archway. The winch meant that the cages could be raised or lowered, so if they wanted to get down safely, that was what they needed to reach. From the mouth of this smaller arch, a narrow ledge circled the cavern, where the burning torches had been lit to flicker at the feet of the huge statues. Thaddeus turned awkwardly, following where it went, and saw, at the opposite end of the cave, another smaller entrance with a narrower sloping path. This path led down to the cavern's main level.

Thaddeus finally let his eyes drop to what filled the space between them and any hope of freedom. Arranged in tight rows that edged the pit and stretched from one side of the cavern to the other were hundreds of people. They all stood, chanting, swaying slightly as if in some kind of trance as they stared wild-eyed at Thaddeus, J, Dita, and Desai. Their faces were the fearsome ghosts that had circled them in the mists: black around the sockets of their eyes, white in the hollows of their cheeks. The men were naked to the waist, wearing loose trousers in a pale, shimmering blue. Each wore a belt that seemed as if it were made of metal that encased his hips and stomach like armor, and into each of these was mounted the sheath of a curved, wide-bladed sword. On these men's chests was a tattoo — a cutlass just like the ones they carried in their belts, crossing over the left nipple where a hard blue stone glittered as it reflected the light of the burning torches. Their arms, all as thick and strong as tree trunks, were clad in impenetrable armor right up to the elbows.

The women — there were as many as there were men — were clad in armored breastplates and wore the same trousers. They too had swords, and each of them bore a tattoo on her left arm, the sapphires glinting and winking, blinding Thaddeus with a thousand pinpricks of starlight until he felt utterly mesmerized by the sight.

The cult of the Sapphire Cutlass.

Chapter 18

A JOURNEY BY NIGHT

$\mathcal{T}$he airship cut through the night, passing swiftly over the dark landscape like a cloud pushed by the winds of a storm. Rémy was impressed with how easily Kai and Upala had become comfortable with the motion of the craft in the air, but then they spent most of their time bobbing up and down in a ship on the ocean. Perhaps, after all, sailing through the air did not feel so very different.

Upala, apparently too restless to sit down, roamed about the cabin, opening cupboards and sifting through what she found there. Kai sat up front beside Rémy. He seemed to be fascinated with the airship's controls, watching closely as she made each adjustment. She wondered whether her brother had half a mind to learn its workings on his own so that he could discard her without keeping to their bargain, but she tried to push the thought away. After all, if you couldn't trust your own kin, who could you trust? And, advisable or not, she couldn't help but want to trust Kai. There was something about him Rémy had warmed to, despite his splinter-sharp glances and occasionally harsh tones. Here on the airship, for example, he was more of a boy than a bloodthirsty pirate, simply fascinated by everything around him. It made Rémy wish even more than she already did that she'd known him as they had both grown up.

"So, Rémy Brunel," Kai said, leaning back in his chair and crooking one leg to rest his foot on the edge of the control panel. "How did you end up traveling the world with a policeman instead of a circus?"

Rémy smiled. "Thaddeus isn't a policeman any more."

Her brother raised his eyebrows. "Even so. A thief and a man of the law? Seems a union most would think unlikely to succeed."

She lifted her chin, staring out into the darkness. "I'm not a thief."

Kai leaned forward to look at her more closely,

elbow on his knee. "Perhaps not *now*," he said, "but I still remember the stories of the circus our father told me as a child. No one could work under that cur Gustave for so long without being put to work."

Rémy grimaced. "Well. That was a long time ago."

Kai leaned back again with a shrug. "Perhaps. So, this Thaddeus Rec. You trust him?"

"With my life."

"It's not your life I'm concerned about. It's your freedom. And mine. I'm a wanted man, little sister. How do I know this isn't some trap to finally put me into the hands of the British?"

"If you really thought that, you wouldn't be here," Rémy retorted.

"Perhaps I like a challenge?"

"Thaddeus is *not* working for the British."

"So he's come all the way here to India to search out an evil that may or may not exist, simply out of the goodness of his heart?"

Rémy leaned forward to make an adjustment to their heading, feeling her brother's piercing gaze on her back. "He came because he knew it was the right thing to do. And . . . because I asked him to."

"Ahh," Kai said. "Now we reach the crux of it. Did you lure him away from his good principles, little sister?"

"Thaddeus would never abandon his principles," Rémy retorted. "He is too good a man for that."

Kai raised an eyebrow. "Is that so. How did you two meet?"

Rémy didn't say anything for a moment, and then was forced to admit, "He was trying to protect a jewel that I was trying to steal."

Kai laughed softly. "And yet here you are, little sister. Free as a bird."

"I helped him return it, in the end, and I haven't stolen anything since." Rémy turned and looked at him. "I will never steal anything again, because of him. I will never *want* to steal anything again, *because of him*. Which actually makes him a rather good policeman, don't you think?"

They stared at each other for a moment. Rémy detected something in Kai's eyes, just for a moment — something like a flash of sadness that was there for no more than a second before melting beneath a wolfish smile.

There was a clatter behind them. Rémy turned to see that Upala had wrenched most of their meager belongings out onto the floor.

"What are you looking for?" she exclaimed. "We don't have anything worth stealing, you know."

Upala made a scornful noise in her throat and kicked a pile of clothes out of her way. "I do not want your rags," she growled. "We need weapons! Where are your *weapons*?"

"We don't have any. We can't afford them."

"Agh!" Upala threw up her arms in exasperation. "Well, don't expect me to give you one of my swords," she said. "You can use those little hands and feet of yours again, for all I care, *anukarana!*" With that, Upala threw herself down on one of the small bunks at the back of the cabin, her arms crossed dramatically over her face.

Rémy turned to look at Kai, who was watching Upala with another grin on his face.

"I wish she wouldn't call me that," Rémy said quietly.

Kai flicked her a glance, accompanied by a slight shrug. "It is as close to a term of endearment as you can expect from Upala."

"Oh?" Rémy said. "In that case, what does she call you? 'The Ugly Real One'?"

Kai threw back his head and laughed. "Perhaps she should, at that."

Rémy couldn't help but smile at her brother's laughing face. "And you two?" she asked, a moment later. "How did you two meet?"

Kai spun back to the control panel, looking out into the darkness as his smile faded. "I found her in the wreckage of a village plundered by the raja's men," he said quietly. "She'd never held a sword before that day. She picked one up and fought like a tiger, but still she couldn't save her family, or her friends. She stood in a ring of blood and bodies, some the raja's men, the rest the people she loved. She thought we were there to take more from her, and she would have killed us too. I asked her to join us instead. That was four years ago. She's been with us ever since, and that tiger has never left her, not in all that time." He lifted one hand to his temple, rubbing at an imaginary spot there. "I don't think it ever will. She is all tiger now. She is all terror."

"Not all," Rémy observed quietly. "I have seen the way she looks at you."

She saw a brief flash of red coloring her brother's neck as he glanced at her from the corner of his eye. "Don't let her hear you say that," he advised. "She'd have your guts for garters. Besides, there is no time in the life of a pirate for that kind of nonsense."

Rémy was about to point out that you have to make time for such things, when something loomed out of the darkness ahead of them. It was the huge, jutting rock promontory where the airship and her original occupants had stopped for the night.

"We are not far away now," she said, leaning forward as they flew over the outcrop. "We will reach the valley soon enough."

Kai leaned forward alongside her, cursing under his breath at the night outside. "When I meet your friend J, I shall ask him why he did not put lights on the outside of this thing."

Rémy grinned. "Ach," she said, "where's your sense of adventure, big brother?"

He glanced at her, amused. "I am saving it for when I need it most."

Rémy's smile faded as she banked the airship and headed for the valley, which even in the darkness surrounding them, showed up like a slash of deeper black on their horizon. At its head, the mountain pricked the night sky, its jagged, rocky edges as immortal as the legend that told of its creation.

"When I left the others, I landed outside the valley for fear of alerting its inhabitants," Rémy told Kai, "but now . . ."

Kai nodded at her unspoken words. "Now, speed is our best advantage, not secrecy. Perhaps you are right. And perhaps the night will conceal us long enough to land."

"Assuming," came Upala's dry voice, speaking so unexpectedly close to Rémy's ear that it made her jump, "that we can see well enough to find a spot to land."

Upala had crossed the cabin floor in complete silence, and Rémy found herself wishing for that kind of stealth. "I will do my best," she muttered as the valley edge grew ever closer.

The pirate woman dropped something small but heavy into Rémy's lap. It was the little axe that usually hung beside the ramp to sever the airship's guide ropes. "It is not a sword," Upala shrugged. "But it is better than nothing. Stick it into that belt of yours, *anukarana*."

Rémy did as she was told, taking her eyes off the controls for a moment as she slipped the axe into her utility belt. When she looked back up at the darkness again, something caught her eye.

"What's that?" she asked, pointing.

Through the window, moving from the west, was a line of yellow lights. They were headed for the valley, just as the airship was — a procession of flaming torches, moving as if they were being carried on horseback.

Kai stood and leaned over the controls, peering

out to get a better look. "Soldiers, perhaps?" he asked. "The raja's men?"

Rémy bit her lip. "They did follow us when we fled the palace. He wanted the airship."

Kai looked at her over his shoulder with a frown. "Well, he's not getting it. It's mine."

"Don't worry," Rémy told him. "They can't reach us up here, and we'll be far ahead of them by the time we land."

Kai still seemed troubled, watching the progress of the lights as they wove through the jungle. Rémy stayed on course for the valley, noting that a thick fog seemed to be lying amid the trees enclosed within its walls. Upala leaned close to her.

"You think you will be able to find somewhere to land in all that?" she asked. "You had better be good at this flying thing, eh, *anukarana*?"

"I will try my best," said Rémy.

"Your best may not be good enough. Perhaps we should set down outside the valley and walk in. If we don't, we risk damaging the ship — and ourselves — on the trees as we come down."

"If we land before we get to the valley, those men down there will find us, or the ship, or both," Rémy pointed out. "Better that we fly into the valley. The fog is a good thing. It'll hide us. And that is what we want, yes? To get as close to the mountain as we can without being seen?"

Upala turned to Kai. "Captain? What do you think? Land here, or land there, in the fog?"

Kai turned, a frown on his face. He was about to speak when, behind him, a light arched into the frame of the darkened window behind him. It burst toward them in a shooting star of flickering yellow flame.

"*Mon dieu!*" Rémy cursed, wrenching the airship's control around, trying to pull it out of the way. Kai and Upala stumbled against each other as the ship jerked and bucked. "They are shooting at us!"

The men below were firing at them with burning arrows. Another lit the night sky, curving past briefly illuminated trees and hurtling toward the airship like man-made comets.

"I thought you said the raja wanted the airship!" Kai shouted, gripping the back of the chair as Rémy swung them this way and that. "Why would he try to destroy it?"

"Perhaps these are not the raja's men after all! Or perhaps he has changed his mind. Whoever they are, they want us to burn," shouted Rémy as the night sky lit up with a myriad of burning arrows. "I cannot dodge them all — there are too many!"

"Bring her down," Kai ordered, his voice shaking as the airship juddered with the effort of avoiding the flames. "Get us out of the air!"

Rémy gritted her teeth and put the airship into a fast plunge. They were nearing the valley's edge and she aimed straight at the fog beyond — if they could reach it and land, there was still a hope that the men pursuing them might not be able to find them there.

The ground came up fast, the darkness giving way to a dense floor of treetops, cut asunder by the valley's sharp edges.

"We'll make it," Kai hissed, "Just a little farther . . ."

Something hit the glass in front of them — a bulge of flame that glanced off the hard surface and spun away, back into the night. For a second Rémy was relieved — that was the closest any of the arrows had come and it wasn't close enough — but then a light bloomed, bright as day against the hull.

"What is it?" she cried, fighting to hold the airship steady in her swift descent. "Are we burning?"

Kai lunged forward, trying to see out of the window as the glow grew. "It's the ropes holding the balloon," he told her. "That last arrow must have lit them. They're going up like fuses!"

There came a vicious jolt that pulled the airship

to one side. Rémy felt the control lever under her hand slacken, spinning uselessly against her hand. The ground was coming up, faster and faster, and she could hear the flames now, roaring in their wake as they ate more and more of the hull.

They were a comet, burning across the sky. They were a meteorite, plummeting to earth.

Chapter 19

TAKEN BY SPIRITS

The airship caught the top of a tree, branches cracking and crunching as they broke and scraped against
the underside of the burning hull. There was a roar, a
rushing bellow of movement from above, and Rémy
knew the flames had reached the balloon.

"We have to get out!" she screamed to Kai and
Upala, even as the ship careened onward, smashing
over the top of another tree, the glow from the inferno
they carried turning the dense, rising fog they rode
into a strange kaleidoscope of refracting colors.

"We're still too high! If we jump now, we'll die,"
Kai shouted.

"If we don't jump, we'll burn!" she shouted back

over the noise of the airship tearing itself apart around them. Lurching out of her chair, Rémy wrestled her way across the bucking floor toward the hatch. "Help me!"

Upala was by her side in an instant, wrenching on the wound ropes that held the hatch shut. Kai made his way toward them, stumbling to his knees as another tree slowed their troubled descent by smashing itself against the airship's nose. The window shattered, shards of glass piercing the air along with a wash of fierce heat.

Rémy pulled at the ropes, ignoring the slicing pain as the glass splinters peppered her back. Upala turned away, hiding her face from the worst of the shards, but Kai caught one full in the cheek, a nasty blow that opened a fresh wound on his scarred face.

The hatch came open, flinging itself away from them as if in a fury all of its own. It tore itself off its hinges, smashing against another treetop, catching against the branches and wrenching itself loose from the hull. The airship followed, twisting around as it lost another part of itself.

The crackle of flame burst from behind them anew, and Rémy turned her head to see fire seeping through the walls as the planks burned through.

"Go," she shouted to Kai and Upala. "We have to go now! *Go!*"

Upala leapt, disappearing into the smoke and fog swirling outside just a second before Kai followed her.

Rémy battled her way across the airship's heaving floor, clinging to the doorframe as the craft bucked and juddered. Its bones were showing now, the planks fracturing, separating, turning to cinders. Rémy thought about the ruby, still in its mooring, but it would have to rest in the ashes, for she'd never be able to reach it without burning herself alive. Outside the fog was so thick it was impossible to tell how far she would have to jump.

The airship smashed into another tree, groaning as if it were in pain, and the cabin split in two.

Rémy jumped.

The fog swallowed her whole, cold and cloying as if she had leapt into a roiling ocean. She tried not to tense up — the only way to survive a plunge from the wire was to let every muscle and bone relax — but not knowing how far she had to fall made that difficult. Branches hit her first, scratching at her face and legs, but mercifully slowing her down.

And then, the ground.

She crumpled, ankles folding to her knees, knees

folding to her hips, arms just managing to stop her head smashing hard against the earth. The breath was knocked from her lungs as surely as she'd been punched in the stomach. Rémy lay on her back, staring up into a mess of swirling gray, lit from above by the flames of the dying airship. They bloomed yellow and orange and red like a sinking summer sun, the colors diffusing through the mist until it felt as if they filled the sky.

Winded and unsure of how badly she'd been hurt, Rémy realized she had to move. The airship was disintegrating above her, raining fire through the fog. A clod of burning plank thudded into the ground just inches from her head. She dragged herself up, feeling a sharp pain in her ankle but ignoring it. Rémy pushed through the mist, stumbling into tree after tree, blind in the gray-white gloom.

"Kai?" she shouted, crunching into yet another tree. "Upala?"

Her voice seemed to echo against the thick mist. Something brushed against her — not a branch this time. Something else. A hand? She spun, trying to follow the movement, but it disappeared before she could fix on it.

"Kai?" she shouted again. "Are you there? Upala, can you hear me?"

A hand clamped over her mouth from behind. She was dragged to the ground, falling against somebody who held her firmly from behind.

"Ssh," hissed a woman's voice into Rémy's ear. "Be quiet, *anukarana*. They will hear."

Upala! Rémy struggled against the pirate's hand until the woman let her go. Rémy scrambled away, turning to face her. Upala held a finger up to her lips and then moved the same hand in a circling motion, indicating the fog around them.

"They are out there," she said quietly. "They are coming for us. They took Kai."

"What? Who? Where —"

A look of irritation flashed across the pirate's face. She leaned forward and clamped her hand over Rémy's mouth, eyes flashing fire as surely as the airship through the fog. Then she froze. For a second neither woman moved at all, until Upala slowly turned her head. Rémy followed her motion with her eyes and saw a movement through the gloom, illuminated by the flames from the still-burning airship. It was barely there — a hint of a shape through the mist, the lithe movement of limbs disappearing into the fog. Upala looked back at her, then removed her hand.

"I saw them take Kai," she mouthed, her voice

barely there. "One moment he was beside me as we looked for you, the next . . ." She flicked her fingers. "We will be next."

Rémy glanced around, detecting more shapes in the mist. Was that a face, there, in the shadows? She reached for the axe and found it gone. It must have slipped from her belt as she fell. Rémy, dismayed, looked at the ground around her feet in case it was there — without the axe she was entirely defenseless. There was nothing. It was gone.

The shapes crowded toward them, closer and closer. There were so many of them, too many to fight, but that wouldn't stop Rémy trying. She'd be damned before they took her so easily. She pushed herself slowly to her feet, feeling Upala move with her and hearing the sound of metal sliding against metal as the pirate drew both her swords. A second later Rémy felt something brush against her right hand. She jerked her fingers away, imagining a creature from the mist grasping at them.

"Take it," Upala hissed.

Rémy looked down to see the woman's hand outstretched, holding out the same blade she had offered her on the beach.

"We will fight them together. Yes, *anukarana*?"

Rémy didn't need telling twice. She grasped the hilt of Upala's sword. "Yes," she said. "Together."

"Back to back," Upala murmured, turning slowly so that their shoulders were touching. "Keep your head up. Do not let them see your fear. Understand?"

The light from the airship was dimming, but even so it was enough to let the two women see what was coming for them. There were figures in the mist, many of them, a circle of bodies joining around them, layer upon layer of them all slowly moving forward. Rémy's heart beat hard — even with Upala's sword in her hand she could see no way of fighting off so many attackers.

Then, above the crackle and spit of the airship's dying throes, another sound grew into the air. At first Rémy thought it was just her heart, beating so hard and so fast that it had set the air alight. But the beat slowly grew: *louder, faster, louder and faster.*

Drums. It was the sound of drums.

The sound thundered through the forest, echoing between the trees and glancing off the mist. At the sound of them, the figures in the mist began to slink away. It was hard to tell at first, so hidden were they by the fog, but one by one, they vanished like wraiths into the forest.

"They've gone," Rémy said, speaking over the sound of the drums.

"Yes," agreed Upala. "But where?"

The two women turned to look at each other, listening to the sound. It felt as if it were beating through them, vibrating the very ground on which they stood, filling their veins as surely as any rhythmic chant.

"They were following that noise," Rémy said. "The drums were calling them somewhere. *To* somewhere."

Upala nodded, her eyes glittering. "Then we must follow. Don't you think?"

Rémy nodded. "Yes," she said. "I do think."

They took off through the trees, staying close to one another and allowing the beat of the drums to pull their blood in its direction.

Chapter 20

DESPERATE TIMES

Over the sound of the incessant drone of chanting
came another noise: the clang and rattle of metal.
Thaddeus turned to see that down on the stone ramp
below them, another cage was being readied for use.
There came another shout: angry, indignant. A ripple
of movement was passing through the rows of swaying cult members — someone was being dragged,
kicking and fighting, to the cage. That someone had
short dark hair and was dressed all in black. Thaddeus
stared hard.

The new prisoner fought hard, but whoever it was
seemed to be hampered by an injured leg. In the end,
the cult was too strong — four grabbed an arm and

a leg each and carried the struggling figure the rest of the way to the cage and threw it inside. The cage was immediately winched into the air, jerking the prisoner around inside with each pull as it gradually rose to meet the others.

"'Ere," said J, "is that Rémy? 'As she got 'erself caught 'an all?"

Thaddeus had been wondering the same thing, but as the prisoner drew nearer he saw that though the incarcerated may be a Brunel, it definitely wasn't Rémy.

The cage slid into place beside the rest of them. For sure, Thaddeus thought, it could have been Rémy. It was most certainly her twin. The man swinging beside them would have been her mirror image if not for the square stubbled jaw and the faint scars crisscrossing his weather-beaten face. He was bleeding from a shallow cut on his dirt-smeared cheek and his trousers were ripped, showing a nastier gash in his thigh. Breathing hard, the prisoner got gingerly to his feet and looked at them each in turn. Then he shook his head and busied himself by tearing a strip of cloth from his ruined trousers and using it to bind his wound.

"An old man, two children, and a sunburned, thread-bare vagabond," he said with a bark of unimpressed laughter. "I should have known."

"Who are you?" Thaddeus asked.

The man finished tying his bandage and put his hands on his hips. "Can't you tell, Thaddeus Rec?"

"You must be Rémy's brother," Thaddeus replied, "but beyond that you have the advantage over me, Mr. . . . ?"

The man stared back at him with eyes that were disturbingly similar to Rémy's. "Kai," he said. "My name is Kai."

"Where is she?"

Kai glanced around with narrowed eyes, taking in the room. "On her way here, I would think."

"As a prisoner? Or free?"

Kai's eyes met his again. "That's to be determined. For our sakes we'd better hope that both she and Upala are still the latter."

"Upala?" It was Desai who asked the question this time.

Kai flicked his glance toward Desai with a serious look on his face. "Upala. She's a gem, that one. If they're both still free, then we may have a chance."

"Wot about the airship?" J piped up. "Is she bringing that, too? I 'ave a feelin' we ain't gettin' out of 'ere without it."

Kai looked at him seriously. "You're J," he said. "She told me you built it. Was she lying?"

J puffed his chest out, scowling. "No, she ain't lying. I got it to work."

Rémy's twin smiled. "I'm impressed." Then his smile faded. "I'm also sorry to report that the airship is no more. We were brought down by fools with flaming arrows. The very last of it is probably still burning out there now."

J's face turned pale and his shoulders slumped. "Burned?"

"Aye. We came in like a sack of rice hurled from a cargo ship. We're lucky any of us survived the crash at all."

"But — but you all did?" Thaddeus asked, fear curling like smoke around his heart. "Rémy wasn't hurt?"

Kai looked at him thoughtfully. "Actually, now you come to mention it . . . I didn't see Rémy leap from the ship. But surely you know by now that she has more lives than a cat?" He grinned. "She and I, we both do. She'll have made it."

Thaddeus rubbed a hand over his face, trying to swallow his distress. He felt Kai's curious eyes on him, but Thaddeus didn't meet his gaze again. A moment later, Kai turned his attention to Desai.

"So you are the one who filled their ears with children's stories, are you?"

Desai raised an eyebrow at the implied accusation and then lifted one arm and swept it out to indicate the rows of swaying cult members below them. "Children's story or not, I would say my prediction of trouble was accurate, wouldn't you, Mr. Kai?"

Kai followed his gesture and narrowed his eyes again. "It's just Kai," he said. "I'm no English *gentleman* and I won't be treated as such." He thrust his chin at the men and women below. "That armor. It's not just armor, is it? There's something . . . strange about it."

Thaddeus had to agree. "I think it's grafted to their bodies," he said, pushing his worries about Rémy to one side. "Look at where the rivets have been placed at their joints. I don't think they can take it off."

"What's the good o' that, then?" J asked. "Won't their skin just be all manky underneath, like? Why wouldn't they want to take it off?"

Thaddeus didn't have an answer for that, except . . . "We saw something similar in France. And in England, come to think of it. Mechanical soldiers."

"But these ain't mechanical," J reasoned. "They's people. Ain't they?"

"Maybe they are at the moment." Thaddeus looked up at Desai with a frown. "But maybe they won't be for long."

Desai's face was serious as he nodded thoughtfully. "There is alchemy that can turn men to stone," he said, "but as for turning them into metal . . ."

"Why turn men into metal," Kai asked, still looking out at the mass of people below, "when you can simply cover them in it?"

"Metal men have no thoughts of their own," Thaddeus pointed out. "They'll do whatever they're ordered to, however terrible the order. They are automatons."

Kai looked down at the chanting army below with a shrug. "You think those men and women down there won't obey any command they are given?" he said scornfully. "Whatever minds of their own they once had are long gone. They are already automatons, Thaddeus Rec. And I bet real people are a damned sight cheaper to find than metal men."

"Then whose command are they taking?" Thaddeus wondered. "They look like worshippers, not like soldiers. Desai, I've been thinking. If you're still telling me this is all for the raja and his mystic . . . I don't think I believe it. Not now I've seen them."

Desai smiled at him thinly. "Ever the detective, Thaddeus Rec. I confess, I was thinking the same thing."

"Well, what then?" Dita's voice made them all look toward her. She was pale, her face fearful. "What is happening here? And what are they," she nodded in the direction of the people below, "going to do with us?"

The rest of them had no answer for that. No good one, anyway. Below them, the dull droning of the chant went on and on. It felt like a drug, flooding Thaddeus's mind until he couldn't even think clearly.

"Well, there's no sense waiting around to find out," Kai said, his voice cutting through the fog of noise around them. "We've got to find a way out of here."

As they watched, he climbed quickly and easily to the top of his cage. Thaddeus was reminded of Rémy again — Kai was almost as graceful in his movements as his sister. He shook the hatch at the top of the cage, but to no avail — it was locked fast.

"Anyone got something I can pick this lock with?" Kai called down to them. "I suppose that would be too much to hope for, wouldn't it?"

"Pity Rémy ain't 'ere," J observed. "She's always got that sort of fing on 'er."

Kai smirked. "And there she was trying to tell me that she was a reformed character . . ."

The end of his sentence rang into silence.

The chanting had stopped. Just like that, as if

someone had snapped their fingers or flipped a switch, the noise ended. Every one of the hundreds of people below them fell silent in one single breath.

The change sent a prickle up Thaddeus's spine. The new quiet was so absolute that he could hear his heart thumping in his chest. Slowly he turned and looked down. No one moved. No one said a thing. The cult of the Sapphire Cutlass had lifted their chins and now stared up at the four prisoners in complete and utter silence, their wild eyes wide and unblinking as if they were nothing more than posed dolls on a child's shelf.

A drumbeat began to sound. It reverberated around the cavern in a rumble like thunder. Low at first — slow at first — it grew louder and faster with each stroke.

Thump thump thump thump
Thump-thump-thump-thump
Thump-thump-thump-thump
Thumpthump-thumpthump-thumpthump
Thumpthump-thumpthump-thumpthump . . .

Their cages began to move. They rattled along the track set into the cave roof above them, inching toward the raised stone stage set with the throne that Thaddeus had spied earlier.

"Oi!" J yelled. "Now what?"

Thaddeus looked up at the track above them, illuminated in a way it had not been before the torches were lit. It wasn't leading to the stage, he realized. It stopped short before that. It ended above the darkened pit sunk in the cavern floor, but he still wasn't close enough to see what it held, though whatever it was moved restlessly in the dim light.

"Desai," he shouted to the front of the line of cages. "What is that? What's down there?"

Desai didn't have a chance to answer. A piercing scream shattered the air, loud enough to drown out the drums.

It was Dita. In the cage beside Desai, she was almost as close to the pit as he was. She pointed at what was below them.

Thaddeus peered down as his own cage finally reached the lip of the pit.

Snakes.

The pit was full of thousands of writhing, squirming snakes.

Dita had stopped screaming and slumped to the bottom of her cage, her knuckles white where they gripped the bars.

"Don't you worry," J shouted to her, his voice almost lost beneath the sound of the drums, "Dita, we'll get out of here before — before anyfin' 'appens wi' those snakes. You hear me? Dita? We're all right fer now, ain't we? They can't get us up 'ere. Can they, eh?"

The little girl didn't answer — perhaps she hadn't heard. She was still staring down into the pit as her cage came to a stop above it with the others sliding into place beside her.

"This is getting worse by the minute," said Kai. "We have to do something."

"Like what?" Thaddeus asked.

Kai looked around. Then he threw himself to the other side of his cage. It swung wildly on its chain, bumping into the one in which Thaddeus was trapped.

"Hey, watch it!"

Kai took no notice. He scrambled to the other side of the cage just as it was swinging back into place, forcing it into further motion. This time it avoided bashing into Thaddeus's prison, arching into a wider swing. Thaddeus saw Kai grin as he leapt to the other side of the cage again. The cage swung even more.

"What are you doing?" Thaddeus asked.

"What do you think? Use your brain, copper! Why else would they put us over this pit unless they intend to drop us right into it? If you ask me, we've got until those infernal drums stop their racket."

"So? What is dashing about like a lunatic going to achieve?"

Kai didn't look at him, still moving swiftly from one side of his cage to the other, rocking it wildly. "We can't stop them from dropping us. The only thing we can do is try to change where we're going to land."

Thaddeus watched as Kai's prison swung again. The chain rattled harshly, pulled as taut as it would go as the cage hovered, just for a moment, over solid ground rather than over the pit. If the chain had snapped then, the cage would have crashed to the floor of the cavern rather than down into the writhing mess of snakes.

"He's right!" Thaddeus exclaimed. "Everyone — do what Kai's doing. Do it now!"

{Chapter 21}

DESPERATE MEASURES

The drums led Rémy and Upala to a ruined temple, an intricate stone façade cut straight into the base of the mountain. They crouched in the shadows of the jungle leaves, watching for signs that anyone was standing guard. There was no movement anywhere. The place seemed deserted, though both women knew better.

Creepers had grown into every crack and crevice of the temple's fascia. They wound around the carved pillars like snakes.

"Better not go in the front door," Rémy whispered to Upala, pointing up to a high window. "Do you think you could climb up there?"

The pirate woman flashed her a sharp grin and

before Rémy knew it, Upala was halfway up the wall, using the creepers to reach the window. Rémy followed, impressed by her fearlessness and stealth.

Within minutes, both women were standing inside the temple. The sound of the drums was even louder here, echoing through the dim torchlight that could be seen beyond the open door of the window room. They moved toward it together, checking this way and that before beginning to traverse the passageway outside. There was no sign of anyone at all.

They moved quickly and quietly, pausing at each room to search for any sign of their people. They found none. Instead, the temple was bedecked with all manner of marvels: stone carvings of what looked like a goddess depicted in several terrifying warlike poses. There were piles of precious stones, too — the sapphires from which Aruna had drawn her fame and fable. They glinted in the meager light, calling to Rémy as surely as if they had spoken, but she resisted the temptation to take one.

Upala showed no interest in any of the rooms they passed at all — a strange pirate indeed, Rémy thought, who was not in the least distracted by such unattended wealth. She thought of Kai's story about her, and wondered what kept Upala going — what interested her now that her life was so empty of family. Although, Rémy reflected, her own life wasn't so different. They had both made families out of the people around them.

The drums pounded on, faster and faster. The two women followed the sound, seeking its source. It couldn't be much farther — the sound was like a summer storm now, close and cloying, hovering right overhead.

They turned a corner, and the tunnel they were in ended so swiftly that Upala almost walked straight out into the open. Rémy caught the other woman by the arm and pulled her backward, out of sight. Together they dropped to a crouch beneath a narrow arch that formed the end of the passageway, staring out at the scene playing out in the vast cavern below them.

Rémy found it difficult to take everything in at once. The first thing she saw was the huge carved statues standing in alcoves hewn out of the rock around the walls of the cavern. They were massive and as intricately formed as the stone carvings she and Upala had found on their way through the mountain. These, though, were many times the size, standing on spindly legs and looking for all the world as if they would lurch forward into life at any moment.

The second thing she became aware of was the people. Hundreds and hundreds of people, mercifully all standing with their backs to where she and Upala hid — there were too many to count easily, but their number was dizzying. She felt a hand grip her arm and glanced at her companion to find Upala pointing at something in the room below them.

Five golden cages were swinging unevenly from the ceiling, each filled with a figure that Rémy instantly recognized. Her heart sank. They had found their friends, all right — but how to reach them? Upala squeezed her arm again and nodded with her chin at the great pit they could see in the floor.

"Snakes," she whispered in Rémy's ear. "It is full of snakes. They are about to become a sacrifice."

"A sacrifice?" Rémy asked, horrified. "Who for? What to?"

A movement across the cavern caught their eye. A figure appeared through the archway at the top of the slope that led down to the stage. He took up position beside the winch fixed in the wall. Rémy realized that the chains fixed to it led to the cages, and her heart clenched. A second later, the drums stopped. The silence filled the space, expanding with the final drum-beat, and in it the new arrival spun the winch.

"Swing harder!" Kai's voice shouted, echoing through the cavern. "Harder!"

The cages dropped. Four missed the pit entirely, crashing instead onto the raised stone platform. The fifth, though, had not swung far enough. It crunched down onto the very edge of the pit, bars folding around the ledge so that it rested there. A thin, high scream of terror echoed from it.

"Dita!" Rémy cried.

"Go!" Upala hissed. "Go, go, go!"

The two women ran along the narrow ledge between them and the winch. Below them, Dita's screams rose higher as the cult members rushed forward and tried to dislodge her cage. The man beside the winch saw the two women coming and pulled his blade from his waistband, but it was Rémy who launched the first sally. She parried his sword with a kick, spinning her shoulder into his chest. Upala followed with a slash of her *talwar* that knocked him off balance and also off the ledge.

Together they grabbed at the winch, trying to turn the wheel that would lift Dita's cage. It was heavy and stiff, so much so that Rémy thought it wasn't going to move at all. Below her she could see more of the cult members surging forward, some joining the cause to push Dita's cage into the pit, others clawing their way up the stage wall like ants. Thaddeus, Kai, Desai, and J had squeezed out of their damaged cages, and J was leaning over the edge of the pit as if he could reach Dita himself, while the others tried to keep the rest of the cult at bay.

The winch gave just as Dita's screams reached a crescendo and the cage toppled into the pit. Rémy and Upala spun the wheel, rushing to take up the slack as it thundered over the edge. In truth, Rémy thought they were too late. The cage disappeared from view, and she imagined it crashing to the bottom, snakes writhing up and around Dita in a slithering morass. But then the chains pulled taut and the winch bit back, raising the cage precious inches.

"There's no time," Upala managed through gritted teeth.

She was right. Some of the cult members who had made it onto the stage were ignoring Thaddeus and the rest in favor of heading for the slope. Upala threw the winch lock and grabbed her discarded sword, turning to Rémy.

"You go help them," she hissed. "I will find a diversion — a way to stop the rest."

"How?"

But Upala had already spun away, and another scream from Dita drew Rémy's attention back to the pit.

Kai, Thaddeus, and Desai were trying to hold off the cult horde by kicking back as many as they could before they made it up onto the stage, but it was hopeless. Kai was already grappling with one and many more were behind.

Rémy looked around. There was no way she'd be able to fight her way down to them. She'd have to help some other way. She looked at the chains that had held the cages in place. They formed a bridge right over the heads of the army below. She couldn't walk them like a tightrope: they were at too much of an angle. But she could climb.

She leapt onto the winch and leaned forward, gripping one of the chains with both hands and pulling herself up, hand over hand, foot over foot. Rémy moved as quickly as she knew how. As she got higher, Dita's cage came into view, swinging slightly as it hung low in the pit. It hadn't touched bottom, but it was very close, just a few inches from the base. Dita had clawed herself as high up the bars as she could and was clinging to them, trying to keep her legs above the snakes that writhed and slithered just below.

The drums started again as Rémy reached the hook

in the ceiling. The beat inspired a surge in the cult members, as if the sound had renewed their energy. They climbed onto the stage doubly fast. Rémy could see her friends backing away, herded into a smaller and smaller space with their broken cages at their backs.

Dita or Kai — who should she go to first? Rémy felt Upala's sword in her belt and knew the answer. Taking a deep breath to steady herself, she wrapped her booted feet around one of the chains that led to the ground. Then, keeping her hands loose and wishing they were gloved, she slid down it. The clang as she landed on the downed cage was loud enough to make Kai and Thaddeus turn toward her.

"Rémy!" they both shouted.

Rémy leapt to the stone floor and drew Upala's sword from her belt, thrusting it toward Kai as she passed him. He seemed to be limping but, even injured, her brother would know how to use it better than Thaddeus could.

Rémy ran toward where J was still leaning over the pit. Rémy didn't even pause before she jumped, soaring past him and landing on top of the cage. The girl was still holding on, but she wasn't high enough. The snakes were winding themselves around the bars, slinking higher and higher.

Rémy dropped to her knees above the girl, tugging at the locked hatch to no avail. "Dita," she urged, "climb! Climb higher!"

"I can't!" Dita sobbed. "My arms aren't strong enough!" She was pale, tears streaking her face.

"You can do it," Rémy told her. "You must!"

"I can't!" the girl wailed again, too terrified to make herself move.

"All right, all right," Rémy soothed. "I will help you. You can do this. *D'accord*?" She quickly undid her belt and then climbed down the side of the cage herself to loop it through the bars and around the girl.

"Remember what we have been learning, Dita," she said to the terrified girl as they faced each other and Rémy fastened the belt. "A little at a time, yes? I am here. You're not going to fall. Take it slowly. Do what I do. We will climb back up together, *d'accord*?"

Dita nodded through her tears. Then she took a deep breath. Rémy began to move, slowly and purposefully, her feet braced against the bars, one hand holding on to the belt, the other grasping at the cage. She moved one foot and then another, a few inches at a time before pausing to let Dita do the same. When they got to the corner of the cage, Rémy had to undo the belt, but Dita clung on until she'd done it up around her again.

"You've done it!" Rémy shouted over the maelstrom of noise around them. "You're at the top. Look, Dita! The snakes can't reach you here!"

Dita smiled and hugged her through the bars, hard. It was only a temporary solution and the belt wouldn't support the girl forever, but it was something.

Rémy looked up to see Thaddeus struggling with a woman who looked as if she could snap him like a twig. As Rémy watched, he dodged backward as the woman swung her razor-sharp cutlass. For a second she thought he'd been sliced through the stomach, but then Rémy saw that it was only his shirt that had been a victim — this time, anyway.

Come on, Upala, Rémy thought. *Whatever you're going to do, do it!*

"You have to help them," Dita shouted to Rémy through the bars. "I can hold on now. They need —"

Dita's words were swallowed by a sound so loud that it even drowned out the noise of the drums. It was the crash of thunder trapped inside a room, accompanied by the creak of a tree big enough to hold up the world falling to its death. The noise drowned out everything else that was going on around them, and the crash that followed shook the ground.

Rémy, still holding fast to Dita, twisted around to see that one of the huge stone statues had toppled from its alcove. The colossus had smashed into the stone slope and had begun to roll down it, crushing everything in its path — cult worshippers and pieces of the cavern alike. Rémy watched open-mouthed as another statue began to fall just like the first, rocking in its alcove for a moment and then, as if in slow motion, toppling forward into the cavern.

{Chapter 22}

A DIVERSION

*W*hen the sound came, it was so loud that at first Thaddeus thought the roof was caving in. His momentary distraction was enough for the woman in front of him to smash him to the ground. He had to scramble back to avoid the blade that followed the blow.

As he fought his way back to his feet, Thaddeus saw one of the huge stone figures set into the walls around the cavern toppling forward, its limbs crumbling into chunks of rock the size of boulders as it went. It crashed to the ground, cracking the surface of the slope before what was left of its body began to roll down toward the platform. As he watched, another of the statues began to fall, smashing into the first.

At this impact the second statue fractured, limbs cracking and splintering into stone dust and shrapnel as the two colossal forms battled for space as they rolled. They picked up speed despite their size, crashing against each other, urging one another on as they hurtled down the slope.

At first the cult worshippers seemed entirely oblivious, too intent on their human foes to notice what was happening behind them. The woman struggling with Thaddeus battled on, regardless. But then something began to happen. One by one, the soldiers turned toward the approaching statues. They raised their arms and walked forward, armored limbs outstretched before them even as they stood in the path of the immense stone tide.

The woman trying to kill Thaddeus abruptly abandoned her attempt. She turned away, walking back to the edge of the platform and quickly descending it. Joining the other cult members, she raised her arms and began to walk toward the statues.

"What's happening?" Kai shouted, and Thaddeus realized that he, Desai, and J had also all been left alone.

The cult members began to chant again. They stood, most of them three-deep in a row that blocked off the end of the slope from the platform. The first row dropped to their knees, arms outstretched, the second leaned over the shoulders of the first, their arms also outstretched. The soldiers in the third row, made of the tallest of the masses, remained upright, reaching out over the heads of the first two rows, also with their arms outstretched. The statues continued their journey down the slope, each smash of their stone bodies sending more and more dust and sharp chips of rock into the air. The cavern was full of it, as thick as the mist had been out in the forest.

"Look!" J shouted, pointing through the smog at the wall where one of the statues had previously stood. "Who's that? She ain't dressed like the rest of 'em!"

A lithe figure slipped out of the now-empty alcove, making back up the stone slope. It was a woman, Thaddeus could make out that much, but no one he recognized.

"That's Upala!" Kai exclaimed with distinct relief. "She's still alive. Where is she going?"

"I have no idea, but I believe," came Desai's voice over the sound of crushing, careening stone, "that this is intended as a diversion to help us out of our predicament. In which case we should take advantage of it while we still can. We have to find the source of the power. We have to stop it, *now*."

"What about Dita?" J cried. "We can't just leave 'er!"

Thaddeus looked over to the cage, still dangling low in the pit. Rémy was working at the lock while Dita clung to the top of her prison for dear life.

"She's all right, J," said Thaddeus. "Look — Rémy's with her."

"She ain't all right!" J cried. "She's still stuck in that thing!"

As if she'd felt their eyes on her, Rémy glanced up and met Thaddeus's gaze.

"Go!" she shouted, her voice only just carrying above the sound of disintegrating rock. "Get out of here while you can! I know how to get us both out of here. I'll take care of her, J. I promise."

"An' who's going to take care of *you?*" J yelled back. "Eh, Rémy? Who's going to take care of you?"

Thaddeus grabbed J's arm, dragging the boy around to face him. "I don't want to leave them either, J, but staying isn't going to help them. If we can work out why this is happening and stop it, then maybe we'll all be saved. We have to go."

"You go," J said, trying to wriggle out of Thaddeus's grip. "Go on. Go. But I ain't going *nowhere*."

"J, you have to. Do you want Rémy to have to rescue you, too?"

"She won't 'ave ter —"

Thaddeus was through arguing. Every second they tarried in the cavern was a second lost for escape. He dragged J away from the pit, though the boy did his best to resist. Kai grabbed his other arm, and together he and Thaddeus practically carried J out of the cavern, heading for the dark recesses beneath the arch at the far end of the platform. Kai was still limping, but if he was in pain, the pirate did not show it. Desai followed behind them.

As they reached the archway that led out of the cavern, a new sound reached them: a rumbling scrape like the magnified screech of chalk scraping over slate. Thaddeus turned to look back, feeling Kai, J, and Desai do the same beside him.

"Bleedin' 'eck," muttered J.

The carcasses of the statues had reached the bottom of the slope. Rather than crushing the rows of cult members, however, they had been forced to a stop by the collective strength of those outstretched, armored arms. As Thaddeus watched, the second statue crashed into the back of the first: an impact great enough to shake the ground on which they all stood. And yet the cult members still stood firm, arms braced against the first statue. They barely even shook.

The chant began again — a rhythmic blend of incomprehensible words rising into the dusty air. Then, so slowly that at first it was impossible to see at all, the statues began to shift. The cult members were forcing the stone monuments to move, rolling their damaged bodies back up the slope.

"Each of those things must weigh as much as my ship with a fully loaded hold," Kai muttered. "How can they possibly be strong enough to move two of them with their bare hands?"

"Their hands ain't bare, though, are they?" said J grimly. "They've got that armored nonsense all over 'em."

"I'm afraid J's right," agreed Desai. "It would seem that their strength is being enhanced already, and I would wager it is not by natural means."

"How can we fight these people?" Kai asked as the sound of stone scraping inexorably against stone went on. "The British Army itself couldn't, rifles and cannon or no. What can we do, with nothing of the kind?"

"We locate the source of this power and we stop it," Desai said grimly. "Now, before it has a chance to grow further."

Kai shook his head with a brief laugh. "As easy as that, eh?"

"You said it yourself, Kai," said Desai. "This is nothing but a children's story — and what is there to be afraid of in that?"

"I'm not afraid," Kai told him. "I just know when I've met my match. So I plan on finding Upala, getting out of here, and taking my ship far, far away where none of this nonsense can find us. The rest of you can come if you want. Or not — it's up to you."

"Wherever you go, be it to the ends of the earth or even beyond, it will not be far enough," Desai told him. "Once this power reaches its zenith and escapes this place, there will be no stopping it."

"I don't know what it is you're looking at, old man," said Kai, "but I'm telling you, there's already no stopping it."

"And I am telling you that you are wrong," said Desai. "Sahoj is behind this, and he may be a mystic but he's still a man, and at this moment he can still be stopped. Trust me, if not we would all be dead already. So this moment is all we have. If we do not act now, *then* all will be lost."

Kai stared at Desai for another moment, as if weighing a mess of odds in his head. Thaddeus could almost see the cogs working in the man's mind as his dark eyes flickered in the gloom.

"You came with Rémy to help," Thaddeus said softly. "No sense in leaving a job half done, is there?"

Kai glanced at him. "Actually, I came because she promised me the airship," said the pirate. "And a fat lot of good that thing turned out to be in a fight."

"Well, then I suppose you have a choice to make," said Thaddeus. "Leave your sister behind and try to make a run for it, or stand up for something. I already know what Rémy would do in your place, however hopeless the situation. She's already doing it, trying to save Dita instead of just her own skin."

For a moment Thaddeus thought Kai might swing the sword he was holding in his direction, but then the pirate shook his head. "You're all fools." He looked at Desai. "All right. Lead on, old man. You'd better know what you're doing, that's all I can say."

Thaddeus paused for a moment, looking back to where Rémy still labored with the lock on Dita's cage. Then he followed, too.

Chapter 23

A BRIEF REPRIEVE

*T*he lock just wouldn't give. Rémy cursed under her breath and glanced down at Dita. The little girl was holding onto the bars, her knuckles white where they gripped the metal.

"You can't do it, can you?" Dita asked, her face a brave mask despite the fear in her eyes. "You can't get me out."

"I'll get you out," Rémy told her firmly. "I promised I would, and I will. I'm going to open this lock, and we're going to use the chain to go back the way I came. All right? Simple. Everything will be just fine, you'll see."

"But —" Dita stopped and bit her lip.

"What?"

"The belt," said Dita, "I can feel it slipping . . ."

Rémy glanced down to see that the ancient leather was beginning to split with the strain of holding Dita's entire weight. She held in another curse and tried the lock again. It wasn't like any mechanism she had ever seen before — it seemed to have cogs within cogs, as if it were operated not by a key but by something else entirely.

"I don't think I can hold myself up," Dita told her. "Not if it breaks. I don't think I'm strong enough."

"Hey," Rémy told her, "don't worry. I'll have you out of there long before that happens, *d'accord*?"

Dita nodded and tried to smile. Rémy smiled back, hoping that the gesture met her eyes well enough to hide the worry that must be lurking there. Even if Rémy did get her out, where were they to go? With the statues dealt with, the pit was once again becoming surrounded by the soldiers of the Sapphire Cutlass. It would take a miracle to get them out of there at all, let alone in one piece.

A shriek from below her brought Rémy's attention back to Dita. With a ripping sound, the belt tore in two. Dita clutched herself closer to the rungs, forcing her feet through the bars so that she could use her ankles as hooks. Rémy flung herself down and reached through the bars for the girl, clutching her tightly to her chest. A split second later Rémy saw something plunging down through the cage, a cascade of tiny silvery implements catching the light as they fell, bouncing against the metal and spinning one by one down into the pit. Her lock picks. Too late to worry about them now.

"I can't hold on," Dita sobbed.

"It's all right," Rémy shouted over the noise of the cult. They had started to chant again, a dull, droning echo that got inside the skull. "I've got you."

Rémy tried to sound more confident than she felt. With every passing second she could feel Dita slipping from her grasp. Rémy readjusted her hold and felt Dita's grip on her shoulders weakening.

"I'm going to fall!"

"You're not!"

"It's no good, Rémy, I can't . . ."

Dita's sentence was cut short as they both felt the cage move. She heard the chain fastened to the hook not far from her face rattle. Lifting her head, Rémy saw it moving. A few seconds later, she felt the cage swaying as it was lifted slowly from the pit.

"Do you feel that?" Rémy cried, "Dita? I told you we'd get out of here!"

Dita sobbed again, tears escaping the little girl's eyes.

Rémy twisted around and looked up the slope. Through the murk she could just see the figure of Upala, using the winch at the top of the stone slope to lift the cage. Rémy's muscles were tiring fast — she could feel Dita's weight growing heavier and heavier below her, but the cage still wasn't clear of the snakes.

Just a little longer, she prayed silently. *Just let me hold on a few more minutes and she'll be safe . . .*

The cage jerked to a stop, the jolt hard enough for Rémy's remaining grip to fail completely. Dita screamed, scrabbling for something to grab onto as she fell. She crashed to the bottom of the cage, hitting her head against one of the rungs.

"Dita!" Rémy screamed.

Then she realized that there were no snakes to writhe around the little girl's body. The cage had lifted just clear of the bottom of the pit. She was safe, after all — still imprisoned, but safe all the same.

Rémy, breathing hard, jumped to her feet on top of the cage and turned to see Upala battling one of the cult members. Sword to sword they fought along the narrow walkway, until the pirate woman bettered her opponent and sent him plunging back down to the cavern floor. More cult members poured past the fallen figures of the statues, kicking up stone dust in their wake as they charged after Upala. Pausing, she turned to look at Rémy across the chasm of space between them.

"Go!" Rémy urged her, pointing one arm in the direction that their friends had fled. "You can't help us now. Go!"

Upala can't have heard her over the noise rolling around the room, but she understood Rémy's gesture well enough. She hesitated again, as if loath to leave Rémy and Dita alone. But the soldiers were swarming toward her, just as they were toward the pit in which the cage now swung gently on its chain.

The pirate woman raised one hand toward Rémy — a gesture of both apology and goodbye — and then fled through the archway, the cult members surging after her like dogs chasing a fox.

Rémy looked down at Dita, still lying prone in the bottom of the cage, and then at the cult members who had come to stand around the edge of the pit.

There was no way out, for either of them.

"Rémy," Dita called up to her with a shaky voice. "What are we going to do now?"

"Don't worry," Rémy said. "Everything is going to be —"

A sudden yelp of pain cut her words short.

"What?" Rémy asked, worried. "Dita? What happened?"

Dita shook her head. "I don't know. Something . . ." she reached down into her skirts and her face grew pale as she drew something out of the folds of fabric. It writhed and wriggled in her hand until she dropped it through the bars of the cage.

A snake.

"Dita!" Rémy cried. "Have you been bitten?"

The girl looked dazed. "I . . . yes . . . I think . . ." She glanced up at Rémy, her face white and her eyes glassy as they lost focus.

"Dita!"

The girl slumped to her knees.

Chapter 24

A FAMILIAR DEVICE

Thaddeus, Kai, and Desai moved along the wide stone corridor as quickly and as quietly as they could.

"How do you know we are going the right way?" Kai asked Desai, glancing back the way they had come, the sword in his hand primed for trouble.

Desai indicated the narrow channel in the floor that had run beside them ever since they left the cavern. "This must lead somewhere, must it not?"

"That's all you've got?" Kai asked, incredulous. "I was hoping for a little more."

"Such as?"

"I don't know — you're supposed to be the mystic!"

"What is that, anyway?" Thaddeus asked, indicating the channel.

"Looks like it's been made to move somefing, if you ask me," said J. "Whatever it is fits in the channel and gets tugged along, like."

"Indeed," agreed Desai, "exactly what I surmised, too, J. And since whatever it is seems to lead straight into that cavern — the meeting place of what seems to be the cult's core . . ."

". . . then whatever we're looking for is probably at the other end of it," finished Thaddeus.

"Exactly."

"Give yourselves a pat on the back, lads," muttered Kai, "with any luck you'll be able to think us all out of our graves, too."

They reached a fork in the corridor. The channel in the floor led down one avenue in the rock that curved out of sight some way ahead. There seemed to be a glow emanating from beyond this curve, a vague light illuminating the route. The other passageway had burning torches on its walls, spaced far enough apart to cast the rest of the route into deep shadow.

"I says we keep following the channel," said J.

"Agreed," said Desai.

"Seconded," said Kai, "but I —" He stopped suddenly. "Footsteps," he hissed.

He was right. Echoing toward them was the sound of running feet. Kai listened again and then pointed at the fork without the channel. "It's coming from there."

"What do we do?" J asked.

Thaddeus nodded to the other corridor. "If we keep going we can be out of eyesight before they get here."

"But then what if they comes down 'ere too?" J asked.

Kai held up a hand for quiet and then listened with a frown. "That's just one person — there's only one pair of feet," he said. "I say we bring down whoever it is. Maybe they can tell us what we need to know. You go ahead — get out of sight if you can."

They did as they were told as Kai took a few steps toward the second passageway. Positioning himself in the center of the corridor, he assumed a fighting stance with his sword at the ready. The footsteps echoed closer and closer as the rest of them moved swiftly away from the fork, heading for the curve and the light that glowed beyond.

Thaddeus heard a cry of surprise behind him. He turned, afraid that Kai had been overrun. The pirate grappled briefly with someone in the shadows, but there was no sign of him raising his sword.

"Kai!" Thaddeus hissed, starting back up the corridor in the hope of being able to help.

"It's all right," Kai's voice came back. Then he appeared with someone else by his side — the young woman Thaddeus had last seen across the cavern amid a blur of stone dust. "It's Upala."

The woman striding toward Thaddeus beside Kai was impressive — tall, dark skinned, dark haired, with eyes as bright as stars and wielding a sword as sharp as any he'd ever seen. Upala looked him up and down briefly, issuing a nod and a curve of her lips that could almost pass as a smile.

"You are Rémy's policeman," she said. "From England."

"I am."

Upala's clear eyes bored into his. "She is a brave one, that girl."

"Yes, she is. Is she — Where —"

"I lifted the cage. It was all I could do. The rest is up to her." She turned to Kai. "There are more men behind me — I heard them. We should not linger here."

Thaddeus looked back down the passageway. At

the point where it vanished, J was standing, waving his arms. Desai was nowhere to be seen. The two men and Upala hurried toward him.

"You ain't going to believe this," the boy hissed when they reached him.

They turned the corner, and he was right.

The room they found themselves in was pure blue, as if they had walked into the sky itself. The stone around them glittered with a faint internal light, revealing layer after layer of facets stacked one upon the other. The entire room seemed to be one huge gemstone, still in its natural state.

"Sapphire," Upala whispered in awe.

"It looks as if we've stepped inside one of those fings the Professor had knockin' around his warehouse, don't it Thaddeus?" J asked. "The crystal fings that looked like boring old stones on the outside, but when you smashed 'em open . . ."

"Geodes," Thaddeus finished for him. "This looks like the inside of a huge geode."

"Tha's the one," agreed J, his tones still hushed.

Kai moved farther into the sapphire cavern, stooping to reach for a pile of loose gems that were scattered across the ground.

"No," Desai told him sharply from where he had

been silently contemplating the room. "Do not touch a thing. Do not *take* a thing."

Kai looked up at him. "You bring a pirate here and you expect me not to pocket at least one tiny stone?" he asked. "It's not as if this place can't spare one, is it?" He crouched to pick up one of the loose sapphires, a large oblong gem that almost filled his palm with its uneven cut. "Just one of these would pay for the repairs to my ship."

Desai moved to him quickly, knocking the stone from Kai's hand so that it skittered across the ground, chinking quietly as it rolled. Kai stood quickly, facing the older man with squared shoulders.

"Kai," Upala said, her voice soothing, stepping forward quickly to put her shoulder between the two men. "I think we should listen to him, Captain. This place . . . it is so strange . . ."

Kai brushed his hands off on his breeches with a shrug. "True enough. Come on then, mystic. What do we do now? Upala says there are more men coming. We need to act or find somewhere to hide."

"'Ere," came J's voice, echoing from some way off. Thaddeus realized that he'd wandered deeper into the stone room. The boy was looking past a towering crystalline formation of sapphire that masked whatever he was staring at. "You lot might want to come and take a look at this . . ."

The rest of them moved to where J stood. Beyond him was another, larger cavern of pure sapphire, but it wasn't the sheer amount of the stone that had caught the boy's attention. It was what was suspended at the middle of it.

"I don't know about you," J said to the collected group. "But that thing there gives me the right willies."

In front of them was a large sphere, formed of metal filaments — thin arms of gleaming silver twisting against and around each other to create a pattern of abstract, many-cornered shapes. These shapes fitted together like the delicate segments of a stained glass window, though the space between each metal twist was empty. At the center of the sphere was a plinth, and from the base of the plinth it was possible to see conduits of similar metal plunging into the rock below. Another series of tubes led farther into the depths of the sapphire cave, twisting and tangling around each other.

"I have seen something like this before," said Thaddeus. "Desai, this is what Abernathy used to power his contraptions. It's why he stole the Darya-ye Noor in the first place. What is it?"

Desai's face was the most troubled that Thaddeus had ever seen it. "It's a Sakhi sphere," he said, his deep voice somber. "I have never seen one, only heard the theory of them."

Thaddeus stepped forward, looking at the empty plinth. "Rémy had to remove the diamond from it to stop it working," he said, turning to Desai. "But there are no gems in this one."

Desai shook his head. "Look around you, Thaddeus Rec," he said. "Why would you need to place gems inside it when you can place it inside a gem?"

"What's it for?" J asked. "What's it do?"

"It is designed to harness the natural power of ancient stones," Desai told them. "More than that, it will amplify them."

Thaddeus looked around. "Abernathy only had the diamonds — the Darya-ye Noor and the one that Rémy's parents stole from the raja," he said. "He knew that would be enough to power his entire army. If this one is connected to all the sapphires in this room . . . it would be enough . . . enough to power . . ."

"Yes," said Desai. "It would generate enough power to mobilize an army big enough to march on the world."

A new fear bloomed in Thaddeus's heart. "Desai, if there is one here, and if Abernathy had one, too . . ."

"Did you see one at the castle of Cantal?"

Thaddeus shook his head. "No, but that doesn't mean there wasn't one there somewhere. I only saw the main cavern. Abernathy had his secured away — we had to cross a chasm to get to it, remember? Desai, if every one of the people on that list of names you gave me in London has one of these . . . They are all over the planet, on every continent!"

Desai nodded, his face becoming grimmer by the minute. "Just so."

"I might not have any idea what the two of you are talking about," said Kai, "but I don't like the sound of it. Tell us what to do, mystic, so that we can do it and get out of here."

Desai shook his head. "It is not activated."

Thaddeus knew what he meant. "Abernathy's had power flowing all over it, through the sphere's filaments, feeding from the diamonds. This one — this one seems to be dead. So where is the power that the cult already has coming from?"

Desai was examining the sphere with narrowed eyes. "Something is not right . . ."

J huffed a half-laugh. "You're tellin' me."

"If this is the heart of everything, why is it not better guarded?" Desai asked. "They surely cannot be so confident, even here, that they would not post a guard?"

"I am liking this less and less by the minute," Kai muttered. He turned to Upala. "I want you to go. Get out of here — I know you can, you'd be able to find your way anywhere. Get back to the ship and tell them to sail as far away from here as possible. Sail east — I hear the pickings can be good in the South China Sea."

A frown like a cloud passed over Upala's face. "And you? What will you do?"

"I've promised to help these people. To do whatever needs to be done. But I'm beginning to feel it's going to have a price I don't like. A price that I wouldn't ask anyone else of my crew to pay."

"You expect me to leave you here?" Upala asked. "With these strangers, to face Shiva knows what?"

"I expect you," Kai said evenly, not dropping her gaze, "to follow orders."

"We're not on deck now, Kai."

"I'm still your captain. I want you to leave."

"Why? I can help. You *know* I can help. Why would you tell me to leave before I am able to?"

Kai's gaze flickered over her face. "The men will need a new captain. I always intended that it should be you if it ever came down to it."

Upala scoffed. "You talk as if you are dead already."

"Maybe I am, Upala, and —" Kai paused, a twinge of something painful passing over his face. "I don't want you to die with me."

"You're not going to die, and neither am I," the pirate woman told him, reaching up with one hand to pull a chain from beneath her shirt. On it glinted a milky white stone, laced with ribbons of color — an opal. "I am your talisman, remember?"

Desai made a surprised sound and sprang forward, reaching out to gently grasp the pendant around Upala's neck. "You have an opal!"

Upala backed away and Desai let the gem fall back against her chest. "Kai gave it to me. After the *last* time I saved his life. Because I am opal myself, yes?"

"Yes," Desai breathed, a look of realization on his face as he turned to Kai. "*Upala* — opal."

Kai shrugged. "I told you she was a gem, did I not, old man? Did you think I was just using a term of endearment? Do I seem like the type to you?"

"This is wonderful," said Desai, his face ebullient with hope. "My friends, I knew there was a reason that Rémy was given that compass — why it was important she found you, Kai, now of all times. Now we do indeed have a chance."

"A chance?" came a drawling voice from behind them. "A chance to do what?"

The sapphire room filled with soldiers. These were not wild-eyed, armored cult members, but liveried, rifle-bearing men with nervous faces and *pagri*-wrapped heads. In front of them stood a man they had all seen before, but only one of them had the misfortune to know of old. Sahoj stepped forward, looking at Desai with a lazy smile and a raised eyebrow.

"Forgive me if I speak out of turn," he said with exaggerated courtesy. "But, Desai, I do believe your chances have just run out."

{*Chapter 25*}

THE SAPPHIRE CUTLASS

"Sahoj," Desai said, his voice echoing around the sapphire chamber. "What have you done?"

"Done?" asked the mystic, walking toward his old colleague as if he were merely taking a stroll in the park. "Why, nothing at all."

Desai waved at the Sakhi sphere, still standing dormant behind them. "Then what is this? And those people out there in the cavern — the cult of the Sapphire Cutlass?"

"Ah ha," said Sahoj, waving a finger. "You should be more accurate with your words, Desai. Your question should have been, 'What am I *going* to do?'"

Thaddeus could see the tension in his friend's jaw as Desai gritted his teeth. "Don't play games with me —"

In a flash, Sahoj had stepped directly into Desai's space, grasping at the other man's throat with a strong hand. "I will play games," he hissed, "with whomever I choose. You, Desai, are no longer a person of authority. Here, or, I would wager, anywhere at all." Sahoj abruptly let go of Desai and stepped back, a sly smile spreading across his face as Desai struggled for breath. "It really is such a pity. You could have joined me, had you been less obstinate. But now . . . Well, now it is far too late. The Sapphire Cutlass has chosen her cohorts, and you are not among them."

"What do you mean?" Desai asked hoarsely.

"Enough talk," Sahoj declared, turning to the soldiers behind him and waving at Desai's group. "Bring them. Let them see for themselves."

The soldiers' gazes flickered to Desai. They seemed reluctant to move, the fear clear in their eyes. Thaddeus watched as they shifted nervously, remembering how their pursuers had fallen back once their prey had crossed into the valley. It seemed to him that these troops had no more desire to be here than he himself did.

"Do it, you lazy curs," Sahoj barked. "Or I'll see to it that you suffer for your disobedience, do you understand?"

At his words, the soldiers hurried forward, leveling their weapons at the prisoners. Sahoj swept ahead as they herded Thaddeus and the others before them, back through the chamber and beneath another sapphire archway. Thaddeus became aware of noise ahead — the chink and skitter of tools against stone echoing faintly in the eerie blue glow that flickered around them.

Beyond the archway was another sapphire room, though this one was not as deserted as the first they had encountered. Indeed, it was a hive of activity. Two more lines of soldiers — this time the distinctive, closely armored figures of the cult — were working steadily, cleaving chunks of precious stone from a point in the room's wall hidden from Thaddeus's sight by their activities.

Sahoj waved the prisoners and their guards to a standstill, surveying the scene before them with a smile on his lips.

"What is this?" Desai asked.

Sahoj turned to him, his smile broadening. It gave his face a distinctly sinister aspect, Thaddeus thought. "Well you see, my dear Desai, when I first found my way into the mountain, I at first thought of it only as the perfect place from which to restore the raja's power. After all, have you ever seen such gemstones? Such quality, such power? But then after I had spent months visiting its hidden corners, I discovered —"

"Sahoj? What is the meaning of you summoning me like some . . . commoner?"

The voice echoed from the archway behind them, interrupting the mystic's words. Thaddeus saw a flicker of irritation pass over Sahoj's face, quickly replaced with an obsequious smile as he turned in the direction of the sound.

There stood the raja Ikshuvaku, imperious as ever, his hands on his hips and flanked by more of his men.

"Ahh, raja," said Sahoj, opening his hands in greeting and striding toward the jeweled man. "I am glad you are here. Your men had no trouble finding their way?"

Ikshuvaku was surveying the room with interest, reaching out to run his fingers down the sapphire walls.

"Once I had impressed upon them the foolishness of their superstitions under pain of instant death, they had no further problems," the raja murmured. "Well, well, so this is the place that has taken you from my side so often during these last months. I must say, Sahoj, that you have done well."

Sahoj bowed deeply as Ikshuvaku's gaze caught on his prisoners. "What are *they* doing here?"

The mystic glanced at Desai. "I believe *he* has been looking for a way to thwart your efforts, raja. I suppose we should have expected as much. No matter. As you see, he has not succeeded."

The raja grinned, placing both hands on his hips as he strolled toward Desai. "No, indeed Sahoj, I see that he has not."

"Raja," Desai began, moving forward as far as his captor would allow. "You must listen —"

Ikshuvaku raised one hand, flicking his fingers toward Desai as if brushing a bug from his tunic. "I must do nothing, traitor. Other than kill you, of course, once and for all. I should have done it years ago — I always have been too merciful for my own good. Why is he not dead yet, Sahoj? Why are they all not dead yet?"

Sahoj bowed again, so deeply that the sash of his cummerbund brushed the azure floor. "I wanted him to see your final triumph, my raja. I wanted him to witness the futility of his attempts to oppose your return to your rightful place."

"Whatever he has told you, whatever he has promised you," Desai said, his voice echoing into the cavern along with the chink of the men still working the stone, "it is a lie, Ikshuvaku, of that I am certain."

"Come now, Desai," Sahoj's tone was coldly haughty. "It is simply because you cannot conceive of anything but betrayal that you can see nothing but the same in anyone else." The mystic turned to look at the raja. "Ignore him, my lord. He is merely twisted with jealousy and bitterness for your wisdom and wealth."

"Quite so," agreed the raja. "It is so sad to see, Desai. You could have shared in the glory and riches as I return to my rightful place — as I return all *India* to her rightful place — and yet instead, here you are, pursuing your own agenda."

"I assure you, Ikshuvaku, *I* am not the one doing that," Desai spat. "Listen to me —"

"Enough," commanded Sahoj. "Raja, I asked you here to see the crowning glory of our achievements come to fruition. To see the moment that my — that *our* plans are put into action."

The raja clapped his hands together with genuine delight. "Wonderful!"

"First, there is something I must show you," said Sahoj. He looked toward Desai, and Thaddeus saw something pass across the hard planes of the man's face that was hard to read. There was triumph there, it was true, but there was something else, buried deep. Fear, perhaps? It was gone in a second as Sahoj turned and addressed the cult members, still working feverishly at the sapphire. "It is time," he said, raising his voice until it boomed against the gemstone walls. He raised his arms, and at the gesture, every worker ceased their movements, turning toward him. "It is time. Prepare," Sahoj commanded.

The cult members turned as one and stepped away, their movements slow but purposeful, as if sleepwalking. As they did so, what they had been working on was revealed.

The air in the room seemed to become unbearably hot. Thaddeus couldn't breathe. He simply stared wordlessly at what stood before him, every hair on the back of his neck standing up in nameless and abject fear.

"Bleedin' 'eck," he heard J mutter.

Desai, standing at Thaddeus's side, drew in a sharp and fearful breath.

Kai spat a word Thaddeus had only ever heard on the docks at Limehouse, but at this moment found himself heartily agreeing with.

Before them had been revealed a young woman of

perhaps eighteen or twenty. She was standing half inside a column of pure, clear sapphire that reached from the floor of the room to the ceiling above. The workers had evidently been chipping her out of her resting place, as if she had been entirely encased in the jewel itself. She had been freed as far as her waist and stood, arms slightly raised as if in the process of stepping forward. The woman's eyes were shut, and to Thaddeus she seemed to be in slumber, but she was clearly alive — her chest rising and falling as she breathed. She was naked to the waist, the dark skin of her arms and shoulders reflecting the tint of the sapphire. It wasn't until Thaddeus looked lower that he realized with shock that where her legs should be seemed to disappear into the remainder of the sapphire column. Below her hips, there was nothing at all, as if something had rubbed the remainder of her being out of existence.

"What is this?" breathed Ikshuvaku.

"This, my raja," said Sahoj, his tones hushed and reverent, "is the Sapphire Cutlass."

There was a pause, and then Ikshuvaku threw back his head and laughed. "This? This child is the dreaded warrior of the old story? This is the power at which armies tremble? Half a girl-child I could snap between my finger and thumb? You take me for a fool, Sahoj!"

A black look flicked across the mystic's face, quickly replaced with another of his smiles. "Trust me, oh great raja. Once you have seen her true power, you will no longer doubt it."

For a moment, it seemed as if Ikshuvaku would move to touch the woman in the sapphire, but Sahoj blocked his way, an apologetic look on his face. "Please, raja, let us finish our work. She is . . . still at rest, as you see."

As Sahoj spoke, the cult members he had sent away returned from several directions. Some bore armor, which they proceeded to strap onto the woman's chest and arms. Others came bearing coils of filament similar to those that made up the Sakhi sphere, unrolling lengths of it so that it reached into the room from somewhere else — somewhere, Thaddeus felt with uneasy certainty, that would join up directly with the sphere itself. He turned to look at Desai as these men reached the woman and began connecting the ends of the filaments to the armor she now wore.

"Sahoj," Desai said, watching with a pale face, his voice tight. "This is foolishness in the extreme. Stop this, now, before it is too late."

"Too late for what, Desai?" the raja asked.

"Too late for him to rescind his traitorous ways,"

Sahoj cut in, before Desai could answer. "Too late to stand at your side as the Sapphire Cutlass bends her power to your will, my raja."

"Ahh," said Ikshuvaku knowingly. "Of course, of course. Desai, I think I have been patient enough with your various deceits. With this creature's power I will retake my rightful place, with or without your approval."

"Is that what he's told you?" Desai asked. "That he is releasing this power for your benefit? It's a lie, Ikshuvaku. No one can control such power as this place — this woman — possesses. No one! What else has he told you? That once this is done, you will reign supreme? That he is only acting in your best interests? Tell me, Raja, if that is the case, then why did he keep this," Desai gestured at the living statue, "a secret until now?"

The raja raised an eyebrow at Sahoj. "It is a valid question, Sahoj."

Sahoj smiled and bowed deeply. "Master, I would not bring you something I couldn't be sure would work."

The raja nodded. "*Now* you are sure?"

Sahoj moved into another gesture of obeisance. His voice echoed back at them from somewhere near the floor. "Oh yes, my raja. I am very, very sure."

"And why is that, Sahoj?" Desai asked. "What have you done to ensure your own survival? What have you promised the Sapphire Cutlass in order to keep your own life?"

Sahoj straightened to look at his former friend with a look of utter contempt. "You bore me, Desai, as much as you ever did. Now it is time to be quiet." He raised one hand in a dismissive gesture flicked toward their guards.

Desai lunged as the men moved forward. He reached for Sahoj, tearing at the mystic's loose white tunic. It ripped in two, the sound echoing slightly against the blue gemstone around them. The guards wrenched Desai back, but it was too late. The mystic's chest had been exposed.

"That's it, isn't it?" Desai said breathlessly, struggling in his captor's grip. "You see, raja?" he asked. "Do you have one of those? I am willing to bet on my very life that you do not."

There, on Sahoj's exposed chest, was a tattoo. It was of an ornately curved short sword, and where it crossed over his nipple was embedded a glittering stone as blue as the fractured walls around them all.

"Enough!" bellowed Sahoj, clutching closed the ruined garment with one hand and making a violent, slicing motion with his other. "Get them out of here. Take them to the throne chamber. There they will bear witness to what they most fear and are helpless — helpless! — to prevent."

"His plan does not include you, raja!" Desai yelled as he and the others were dragged away. "If it did, you would have the tattoo as well! Only those who have it will survive! She will only recognize those who bear the tattoo as her followers!"

Ikshuvaku took no notice. A new drumbeat began.

Chapter 26

A POISONOUS
TRANSFORMATION

*R*émy was still crouched on top of Dita's cage, the little girl slumped across the bars at the bottom.

"Dita!" Rémy cried. "Stay awake! Can you hear me? Try to stay awake!"

The drums began to sound again. They echoed through the cavern, louder than ever before. The cult members began to move. They abandoned the pit and some left the raised stone stage, dropping back down to the ground level to resume their previous formation. Others remained on the platform, separating into two silent, impenetrable lines. One by one they all turned to face the center of the platform, a fresh chant beginning, droning on endlessly beneath the beating drums.

There was movement behind the stage, too. Out of the darkness of the archway came another cascade of cult members, walking in two slow, solemn lines on either side of the channel etched in the stone floor. Each of these carried a drum, fastened around their necks with a cord woven of blue thread, beating it rhythmically as they walked slowly out of the gloom.

Between them, apparently moving of its own accord within the channel in the floor, was a huge stone throne, patterned with ornate carvings. It was turned away from the cavern, its back so high that Rémy couldn't see who was sitting in it. It slid smoothly in time with the drumbeat, tugged forward by invisible hands. To its left walked a lone man not dressed in the colors of the Sapphire Cutlass, but in white, with a golden cummerbund at his waist and a turban wrapped around white hair — Sahoj. His white tunic had been torn to reveal the tattoo of the cult, etched across his chest. He stared straight ahead, walking calmly in time with the throne until it reached the end of the channel. When it stopped, he stepped aside, turning to face it, a movement echoed by the drummers. They, too, turned inward to face the throne, still hammering out a slow, hypnotic beat.

Rémy saw movement to her right, this time at the

tunnel entrance near the winch. She looked over to see her friends being herded back into the cavern. Behind them were more soldiers, not wearing the colors of the cult this time, but those of the raja. Her friends were trapped, outnumbered, and surrounded, and Rémy's heart sank. Surely, now, all hope for them — for everything — was lost.

The drumbeat ceased, although the chanting went on. She looked back toward the stone stage just as the throne began to rotate, swinging on an invisible pivot.

Rémy felt her breath run still in her chest.

On the throne sat a woman clad in gold, her eyes shut as if she were sleeping. Her chest was encased in a breastplate that reached over her shoulders to end in spikes as sharp as a church's spire. Her armor was etched with intricate patterns — whorls and loops like the waves of a churning ocean so that it seemed to ripple even though she was as still as the statues around her. Her waist was encompassed in a wide belt, also of gold, edged by strands of blue silk that fringed her thighs.

The woman's legs were bare, though at first it seemed as if they were clothed in the same blue silk as worn by her followers. But then, as they caught the light from the flaming torches on the walls, Rémy realized the truth. Her legs were not covered, but transparent, formed of a stone so clear and so blue that it would match the sky of a high summer's day over Paris. Even from this distance, where she clung on top of Dita's cage, Rémy could see how they distorted the shape of the throne behind them, refracting the image of the carved stone as if through a prism.

Slowly, deliberately, the woman raised her hands and then lowered them to the armrests of her throne. She tipped back her head, opening her eyes.

Rémy shivered. Behind the woman's lids there was nothing but pure, bright sapphire, faceted to glint and shine the same unnatural, transparent blue as her legs.

The Sapphire Cutlass pressed her palms into the stone arms of her throne. Rivulets of power began to dart from her form into its carvings, tracing from where her heart should be along the patterns that circled her armored torso and into the throne, as if the chair was part of her. She lifted her chin, and Rémy realized with dread that the supernatural woman was looking straight at the cage on which she crouched. The Sapphire Cutlass moved her head with one tiny flick, and the cage instantly began to move. Rémy felt it judder beneath her feet and then lift clear of the pit before swinging toward the throne and descending, just as smoothly, to land at the woman's feet.

Dita lost consciousness completely as the cage touched the stone. The Sapphire Cutlass stepped from her throne with silent, menacing grace. Rémy flexed her arms and rotated her shoulders, ready to fight. The goddess seemed not to notice her at all, her attention fixed on Dita instead. Rémy sensed her chance and leapt from the cage, left foot extended in a move she would usually use to mount a moving pony in the circus ring.

She was knocked from midair by the metal-clad arm of one of the woman's attendants. Rémy crashed to the ground, a forest of legs closing in around her. She sat up, her head ringing painfully from the impact, and rough hands grabbed her shoulders, dragging her to her feet.

The Sapphire Cutlass seemed oblivious to the disruption. She raised one hand toward the cage, and two of her soldiers moved forward to grasp the bars. Another fluid movement of her hand, and they were pulling the metal apart, bending the rods, prying open Dita's prison as if it were made of nothing more than paper. One of them reached in and lifted the little girl out, laying her at the foot of his goddess.

"Dita," Rémy shouted, struggling against the arms that held her. "Dita, wake up!"

The girl didn't move at all and Rémy feared that she was already dead. The Sapphire Cutlass looked down at the lifeless pile of rags that was Dita, examining her with cold blue eyes. Then, slowly, she crouched at the girl's side and extended one hand to place it on Dita's forehead.

"Stop it!" Rémy cried, still struggling and still trapped. "Leave her alone!"

She saw a tiny lick of blue flame dance around the woman's arm. It circled the limb from shoulder to elbow, from elbow to wrist, from wrist to palm, before flickering out of sight. The Sapphire Cutlass withdrew her hand from Dita's head and stood up. She remained at the girl's side, looking down with her impassive, terrifying blue gaze.

The drumbeat went on and on, crashing and echoing around the cavern. Rémy's head ached and the flames from the ever-burning torches were beginning to hurt her eyes.

Dita moved. She turned her head left and right. She sat up. She opened her eyes.

They were of the purest, purest blue.

They were sapphire.

{Chapter 27}

A NEW JEWEL

$\mathcal{T}$haddeus struggled to hold on to J, who was fighting against him with everything he had.

"Dita!" J cried. "What's that monster doing to 'er?"

Thaddeus felt helpless, watching as Rémy was held fast by two of the goddess's guards. There was fresh movement behind him, and Ikshuvaku appeared, his terrified soldiers parting to let him through. As he looked down into the cavern, the smug look on the jeweled man's face turned first to shock and then to fear.

"What devilry is this?" The raja's horrified voice was so hushed that it was almost lost beneath the pounding beat of the drums.

"What's the matter, raja?" Desai asked quietly. "Not entirely how Sahoj described it when he spoke of the Sapphire Cutlass?"

The jeweled man opened his mouth to say something else, but no sound was forthcoming. After a second he shook his head and tried again. "He told me she would become another servant," Ikshuvaku murmured. "That once she was awake, she would do my bidding and none other's."

Desai's mouth twisted into a grim smile. "Does she look as if she's likely to take your orders, Ikshuvaku? Does she look as if she would take the orders of any mere man?"

The raja tried to say something, but managed only to stutter, "This . . . this power . . ."

"It should not exist," Desai finished for him.

The raja fell silent again, continuing to watch as the Sapphire Cutlass turned her attention to Sahoj. The mystic stepped forward with a deep bow, and appeared to say something to the woman.

"Are her legs truly made of sapphire?" Thaddeus asked, somewhat mesmerized by the play of flame-light that danced through the strange woman's transparent limbs. This all felt unreal, somehow, and he wondered whether that was the point of the never-ending drumbeat, which now almost felt as if it were coming from inside his own skull.

"She is becoming the stone," Desai answered. "See the power that radiates from her even now? When the transformation is complete . . . she will be unstoppable."

"Surely you exaggerate, as always, Desai," said the raja, his tone straining to achieve its usual languid mockery. "Sahoj clearly thinks she can be controlled, or he would not be so close to her."

Desai cast the raja a pitying look. "He does not seek to control her. He seeks to join her — to stand at her side and feed from her fortunes, even as he did with you all these years. Your power is almost spent, but hers is rising and it will be greater than the world has ever seen. What better place to enjoy such power but at its right hand?"

"The tattoo," Kai spoke up. "Is it really so important? They all have them."

"It is how she will recognize her followers and bestow her power upon them," said Desai. "Any without it will serve as slaves — or perish."

"The Comte de Cantal had one," said Thaddeus. "So we have to suppose that all those other people on the list do, too."

"Indeed," Desai agreed. "They have been planning this for years. Decades, perhaps. It seems her followers are spread throughout the world, awaiting this awakening and the power of her true strength. With it, no mortal will be able to stand in their way. They will own the world."

"What do we do?" The words were spoken by the raja. When the eyes of the group turned to him, he squared his shoulders and set his jaw. "I do not have the tattoo. I will not serve and I refuse to die," he spat.

"The only chance we have now is in the opal," Desai said, turning to look at Upala. "It may be the only thing that can stop the transformation."

Upala pulled her opal pendant from beneath her shirt as she looked down at what was happening below them. It glowed faintly in the dim light of the cavern. "What do I have to do?"

"Nothing," Kai said forcefully as he stepped forward. "Whatever has to be done, I will do it." He held out his hand to Upala. "Give me the stone."

"No," said the pirate woman. "You gave it to me. It is mine."

"I will return it to you," Kai told her, gesturing with his hand at the opal. "When this is done, you can have it back."

Upala looked at him steadily. "You are injured," she pointed out. "Whatever has to be done, I am sure it will need to be fast. Tell me, old man," she said, her gaze still fixed on the pirate captain even as she addressed Desai. "What must I do?"

"The opal must drain her power," Desai told her. "To do that you must press it to her forehead and hold it steady. For as long as it may take."

Kai spun to look at him. "You have got to be joking."

Desai shook his head. "I am afraid not."

"You are not doing it," Kai said, turning back to Upala. "I am your captain — it's my responsibility. Give me the opal."

Upala took a step back. "I will not," she said calmly. "The gem is mine. You gave it to me. I accepted it and now I accept the responsibility for using it."

"But I didn't know!" Kai burst out. "When I gave it to you, I didn't know all this. I just wanted . . . just wanted to . . ."

Upala moved closer. "You wanted to . . . what?"

Color sprang into Kai's cheeks. He looked away, putting his hands on his hips and adopting a swaggering stance. Upala lifted one hand and ran her fingers lightly along his jaw. He reacted quickly, reaching up to grab her wrist and clutching it tightly against his chest.

"You are my captain," Upala said softly, "and I am your talisman. I will do this. It is my duty. It is my right."

"You'll never make it," Kai said thickly. "They'll kill you before you even reach the demon."

"Have a little faith, Captain Kai."

He tugged her a little closer. "If I have ever had faith in anything, then I have it in you."

Upala smiled, a spark of bright beauty against the backdrop of nightmare playing out below them. She stepped away from Kai, turning to face the rest of them as the captain's hand released her wrist and slid down to grasp her fingers instead.

"I will need a diversion," she said. "Or Kai's right, I will not make it. Fight like tigers, my friends, and we may still prevail."

"What about Dita?" J asked. "We can't just leave 'er like that! We've got to 'elp 'er."

"Go for the girl first, if you can," Desai told Upala. "Her transformation is new, and you may still be able to reverse it entirely."

Upala nodded. "All right. Now, enough talk. It is time for action." She let go of Kai's hand and drew her sword. "Carve a path that will make them think we are launching a full-on attack."

"And you?" Thaddeus asked. "What are you going to do?"

Upala smiled at him. "I shall take a stealthier route."

She went to move away, but Kai reached out and pulled her back, spinning her toward him. They stared at each other for a split second, and in it Thaddeus felt his stomach drop. He knew that look — he had looked at Rémy that way so many times that it was impossible to count them all.

"Don't die," Kai begged Upala quietly. "That's an order. *Don't. Die.*"

Thaddeus looked away as their lips met. His eyes sought out Rémy instead, her black-clothed figure drowning in the impossibly huge sea of gold and blue that flooded the cavern below, and his heart turned over. These past days and hours had been about the fate of the entire world, and yet in the few seconds of yearning he had felt radiating from Kai and Upala, Thaddeus recognized a simple truth.

None of it mattered to him without Rémy.

{Chapter 28}

LAST CHANCE

$\mathcal{R}$émy found herself firmly trapped between two lines of the cult's soldiers.

"Dita," she shouted, trying uselessly to push between the bodies in front of her. "Can you hear me? Look at me!"

The little girl was on her feet now, her back to Rémy, her hands hanging loosely at her sides. The Sapphire Cutlass was walking back to her throne, and on her back was a new bloom of stony blue, creeping up toward her shoulders from beneath her armor, turning her flesh transparent. The stone in her nature was spreading steadily through her form.

The unnatural woman sat down, more little arcs of

blue electricity snaking from her form to hiss across the stone. She lifted her chin as if surveying the room, and for a moment Rémy thought she was going to say something. Instead, she lifted one hand and held it out to Dita, who began to move toward her.

"No!" Rémy shouted. "Dita! Wait!"

She struggled forward, trying to force her way between the soldiers. They were an impenetrable wall. Hands dragged her back, one arm twisted up and around her neck until she felt the breath struggle to reach her lungs. Rémy kicked out, aiming for her captor's shin and hearing a sharp intake of breath somewhere near her ear. She'd obviously caused some pain, because the grip on her throat lessened a fraction — enough for her to take a lungful of the cavern's musty, stale air.

Rémy dropped her center of gravity, becoming a dead weight as the soldier who had her in his grip tried to regain his composure. She slid farther out of his grasp, dropping to her haunches as his hands scrabbled to pull her back up. That was all the time Rémy needed. She twisted, flicking her hips into a spin just as she would on the trapeze, bringing her lead leg around so fast that the force was enough to pull even further on her captor's upset balance. For a second, she was free, pivoting quickly to bring her left leg up and punch it forward into his unprotected sternum. She felt the crack under her foot as his bones gave way, but it didn't give her pause. She lunged forward, dragging his cutlass from his belt as he slumped to the ground.

Wheeling with a wild yell, she sliced the curved sword around her in a circular motion, sending more of the soldiers out of alignment. The drummers faltered, unable to defend themselves as Rémy leapt toward them. She didn't try to go through them — instead she took a running jump, launching herself at the tallest of the line and planting one foot against his drum as she soared skyward. The leverage gave her enough momentum to take her over his head in a curling twist that landed her several feet in front of him more quickly than he had time to react.

"Dita," she cried again, but the girl acted as if she heard and saw nothing at all but the strange woman seated on the great, carved throne. Rémy ran forward and grabbed Dita's shoulder, spinning her around.

Where Dita's eyes had once been there was only the transparent blue of stone cold sapphire. The rest of the girl's face was entirely expressionless. Then she smiled, a gesture as chilling as the sight of her eyes.

"Dita," Rémy begged. "You must be in there some-where. You must be! Whatever this is, fight it — I'll get you out of here. I promised, didn't I? And Rémy Brunel does not break her promises."

A roar echoed around the cavern. Rémy turned to see a commotion thundering down the stone slope toward them — a whirling rush of faces she recog-nized, together with some she did not. Thaddeus and Desai led the charge, running headlong toward the platform, side by side. She could see J and Kai doing the same but taking a different route, down onto the cavern floor. There, too, was the jeweled man and some of his soldiers, their faces contorted into the screams and yells of battle as they surged toward the far greater force of the Sapphire Cutlass. Of Upala, though, there was no sign.

Around Rémy, the atmosphere instantly changed. The drumbeat became chaotic as some of the drum-mers abandoned the rhythm. The men who had been charging toward Rémy faltered, looking up at these new attackers. The Sapphire Cutlass turned in her throne, her attention captured by the noise as Thaddeus and Desai piled into the first row of soldiers. Sahoj, standing at her right hand, raised his arm, and just as if he had issued a silent order, the cult members around them began to run toward the fight, eager to protect their goddess from the onslaught.

Rémy saw a chance at once — with the attention of the cult and its leader elsewhere, a gap had opened up behind her. She grabbed Dita by the arm.

"Come on," she said urgently. "Dita, we have to go . . ."

Rémy managed to drag the girl a few steps. Then she felt something clamp down on her arm. Rémy looked to see that Dita had grabbed her and was squeezing so hard that Rémy's arm was turning white.

"Dita, you're hurting me," she said. "Let go."

Dita ignored her, staring at her with those transparent blue eyes, a sly smile plastered across her face. She squeezed tighter and Rémy yelped in pain. She tried to twist herself free from the girl's grip, but Dita held fast. Her strength was phenomenal — no matter how Rémy bucked and wove, the girl stood firm. Rémy dropped the cutlass, using her free hand in an attempt to pry Dita's fingers loose, but it was no good. Dita clamped her other hand over Rémy's wrist, drawing her arms together so that they were useless.

Rémy couldn't help but cry out as the pain in her arms grew sharper. Her fingers were tingling, cold — rainbowing from red to blue where the blood supply had been cut off. It felt as if her bones were being crushed under the pressure.

"Dita," she begged, "please . . . stop . . ."

The girl ignored her. Eyes blurred with pain, Rémy kicked out, trying to use her legs as weapons, but Dita parried every blow she struck with impassive ease. Rémy sank to her knees and saw, over her shoulder, her friends waging a losing battle. *It's almost over*, she thought desperately. *We can't win this* . . . Almost as if the Sapphire Cutlass had heard her thoughts, she turned away from the scrum to look at Rémy. Dita looked up at her new mistress, their blue eyes flickering with an unnatural common knowledge. The sapphire had crept to the woman's neck, already tracing its thick lines of stone up her veins to her face. She glittered as she moved, a human body being slowly swallowed by a living, livid gem.

Rémy felt herself tugged forward, her knees scraping against the rough ground as Dita pulled her toward her mistress. Resisting was impossible — Dita's supernatural strength was overpowering. The Sapphire Cutlass raised herself out of her throne once again, this time with all her attention focused on the woman trapped in Dita's clutches.

A flurry of movement surged across Rémy's

now-blurred vision. It emerged out of the dimness behind the throne, from the direction of the tunnel from which the Sapphire Cutlass herself had been brought. Rémy, struggling with the rising pain, only realized it was Upala when the pirate woman arrived in front of her, dropping the sword she had been wielding to clamp one hand to Dita's forehead and wrapping her other arm around the girl's waist.

Dita screamed and released her hold on Rémy. The girl's cry was a howl of pain and anguish. She writhed in Upala's grip, but the woman held on. The Sapphire Cutlass bellowed too, the strange sound of rock grating against rock. The blue bloom of stone had now mottled her face — her lips were pure, undulating blue, her cheekbones were sketched in true sapphire. Upala backed away from Rémy, pulling Dita with her and turning to face the goddess.

Rémy struggled to her feet, grabbing Upala's sword and throwing herself between the Sapphire Cutlass and the pirate woman. She traced the air between them with swift slashes, but the Sapphire Cutlass barely seemed to notice. Her forehead, now almost entirely gem, wrinkled as she frowned, her mouth open in a roar of anger that showed teeth and tongue of solid, moving stone. She dashed away Rémy's sword with nothing more than the back of her hand, as if she were swatting away a fly in the midday heat. She advanced, one firm stride at a time, and Rémy found herself forced back, still aware of Dita's weakening cries behind her.

The Sapphire Cutlass moved swiftly, glittering a trail of light like bursts of fireworks as her hard heels sparked off the stone beneath her feet. Rémy heard a soft thud behind her, and a moment later, Upala was at her side.

"Take the girl," she said breathlessly. "I will deal with this."

Upala grabbed the sword and Rémy let it go. In the fraction of a second before she turned away, the pirate woman fixed her with a fierce look.

"Make sure Kai leaves," she said. "He will want to stay. Make sure he understands — I do not want him to."

Rémy had just enough time to nod, and then Upala was gone, her hair whipping out behind her as she wheeled toward the fight.

Dita was lying on the ground, her eyes closed, her face impassive. In two steps Rémy was standing over her, wary of being caught again.

"Dita?" she asked, but got no answer.

She looked over her shoulder to see Upala and the

Sapphire Cutlass facing each other. Upala raised her sword and spun into a slicing blow that glanced off the woman's armored upper arm, casting sparks into the musty air. The Sapphire Cutlass merely reached out and grasped the blade, closing her gemstone fist around it as if it were nothing more than a blade of grass. She pulled Upala toward her, gathering her into a deadly embrace.

Upala did not resist. Instead she took the goddess by surprise. She hurled herself forward, straight at the once-woman's chest, so quickly that the Sapphire Cutlass had no chance to defend herself. Upala raised her free arm and opened her palm, slamming it against what had once been the woman's forehead.

The sound the Sapphire Cutlass made was more of a bellow than a scream. It roared out of her, sharp and deep, the noise of sheering stone, of an avalanche. A movement shot through the stone of the cavern itself, rippling the air like a flame. The scream went on and on, and Rémy watched, open-mouthed, as the gemstone figure began to shudder and convulse.

A sudden hush fell as in one single, charged second, every member of the goddess's cult realized what was happening. The change was instant. They no longer cared about the men they were fighting. All they saw was their goddess in pain.

"Go," Upala shouted at Rémy, her voice vibrating as the shaking of the Sapphire Cutlass juddered through her being. "Get out!"

The tide of cult members turned. Roaring, screaming, yelling, they all rushed back toward the platform — toward Upala and their screaming goddess.

Rémy spun toward Dita and saw the girl's eyes were open.

The sapphire hue had gone.

"Dita," she said, crouching at the girl's side. "You've got to get up. Can you move?" She tugged the child upright and into her arms. Dita's head lolled against her shoulder, and if not for the fact that her eyes were open, Rémy would have thought she was asleep. "Wrap your legs around me, and hold on."

She staggered upright, taking Dita's weight with her, and ran. Behind her, the sound of pounding, running feet echoed along with the war cries of the cult and the screams of the Sapphire Cutlass. She felt Dita lift her head.

"Don't look," Rémy told her. "Dita, don't look."

Chapter 29

DONE FOR

$\mathcal{T}$haddeus saw Rémy scoop Dita into her arms. Between them, the worshippers of the Sapphire Cutlass were separating, scattering in their confusion and fear.

"Rémy," he shouted, cupping his hands to his mouth to make himself heard over the din.

At the sound of his voice she looked up, their eyes meeting across the distance. A smile bloomed on Rémy's face, blotting out the exhaustion that had shadowed it a moment before. They ran toward each other, ignored by the last straggling cult members that had not converged on the throne.

Rémy staggered under Dita's weight as she reached him.

"Let me take her," Thaddeus shouted, hefting Dita from Rémy's arms.

"What's happening?" she shouted back. "What's Upala doing?"

"She has an opal," Thaddeus told her. "She's our last chance to stop Aruna's transformation."

They struggled back up the slope as Kai made his way toward them, limping badly. The fight had worsened his injury and now blood was seeping down his leg, drops of it rolling in the dust of the cavern floor as he moved. He didn't seem to notice — his gaze was fixed on the fight below. Upala was still locked against the Sapphire Cutlass, her grip refusing to waver even as Sahoj attempted to pry her away with his bare hands and the cult members swarmed her like ants. Blue sparks were exploding in the air above the two women, fizzing and spinning as they arced away from where Upala's brave hand ground the opal against the goddess's sapphire skull.

The ground began to shake. For a second Thaddeus thought it was just the chaos around him, the weight of a thousand pairs of frantic feet pounding on the cavern's floor. But then came another tremor, then another and another, each greater than the last.

"An earthquake," Desai shouted. "It is the power being released from their struggle."

The tremors increased. A tearing sound ripped through the cavern. Below them on the cave floor a split appeared, zigzagging through the rock, a black void opening into the ground. One by one the burning torches fizzled and spat their last, until the only light left spun from the blue trails of electricity thrown from the Sapphire Cutlass.

"We have to go," said a voice. "This place is tearing itself apart!"

It was the raja. The jeweled man looked disheveled. He was breathing hard and his tunic had been slashed by the blade of a sword. Blood ran down his arm from a cut across his bicep. Behind him, his men were fleeing into the darkness, swallowed up by the mouth of the tunnel they had driven Thaddeus and his friends through earlier.

Another rumble of cracking rock and a split appeared in the cavern's ceiling, sending chunks of stone plummeting down into the cavern.

"I'm not leaving without Upala!" Kai shouted over the din. "Go. Go on, all of you. Run. But I'm not leaving her."

Rémy grabbed his arm, turning him to face her.

"She wants you to leave," she told him, voice shaking with the vibration of the earthquake. "Upala knew you would want to stay. She wanted me to tell you — she doesn't want you to."

Kai frowned. "I can't just leave her. Not now. Not here — not like this."

"She wants you to live, Kai. She's doing this so you can *live*. We can't save her. You know that. But if you live — so will she. In here. Yes?" Rémy moved one hand to place it on Kai's chest, right over his heart.

Kai wrenched himself away as the others fled for the archway. Rémy waved Thaddeus off as he tried to pull her away.

"I will follow," she said. "I promise. Get Dita out of here."

"We've gotta go, Mr. Rec," J yelled. "We've got to go *now*!"

Thaddeus turned and ran, cradling Dita against his chest as chunks of gray rock rained down on them. When he reached the archway, Thaddeus chanced a look back. To his relief, Rémy and Kai were following.

★ ★ ★

They staggered along the corridor, straggled out in a wide line behind the raja and Desai, Thaddeus carrying Dita with J by his side, and Rémy with her arm around the hobbling Kai. They made their way through the mountain, shuddering along with the stone itself as the earthquake went on around them. They passed room after room of antiquities that were being shaken like dust from their places.

"I tell you," said Kai, breathless, "if I had known this place was here, they would have lost all of these years ago. What a waste."

Rémy tugged him onward. "Don't even think about it."

Kai stumbled as a tremor shuddered the ground beneath their feet. He braced himself against the wall, casting a grim look at Rémy.

"Think about what?" he asked. "The fact that there's no way we're going to get out of here alive?"

"Don't say that," Rémy ordered him, forcing him onward.

"I should have stayed with her," Kai said, his dark eyes angry, though Rémy sensed the rage was mostly aimed at himself. "We're going to die in here anyway. I should have died with her."

"We are not going to die," Rémy hissed, her own anger surging as she struggled to keep them both moving forward. "And Upala wouldn't thank you for staying."

Kai gave a bark of laughter. "She rarely thanks

anyone for anything. She doesn't have much to be thankful for."

"She has you," Rémy observed.

Kai said nothing to that. Rémy twisted her aching neck to glance at him. The look on her brother's face was closed. There was something excessively sad about it.

He loves her, Rémy thought to herself. *I wonder if he ever told her so?*

Kai looked up and met her eye. He opened his mouth to say something, but whatever the words were, they were lost in the catastrophic rumble of another huge tremor. The force was enough to jolt them apart — Rémy lost her grip on Kai's arm and fell back against the rough rock wall of the corridor hard enough to knock the back of her head against the stone. She slipped to the floor, jarring her tailbone as she blinked, trying to clear the sudden blur in her vision. Kai ended up on his knees, his sharp cry echoing along the passageway as the impact tore at his already-injured leg. Blood spattered from the wound and Rémy saw him clamp one hand over it in an attempt to stop the bleeding.

Another huge tremor immediately followed, shaking Rémy like a dog until her teeth rattled against each other. Ahead of them, Thaddeus was struggling to keep his balance while he held on to Dita, shielding her head with his hands as he tried to brace himself against the shuddering, shaking wall. J had fallen at his feet and was on all fours, trying to get back up. Rémy did the same, but every time she made it to her feet, another seismic wave sent her off kilter again. Kai had curled into a fetal position, one arm trying to protect his head from reverberating off the rock floor, while the other clamped uselessly against his wound.

Rémy shut her eyes. The noise was deafening, as if they were standing inside the barrel of a cannon at the second that its fuse connected with the gunpowder. It rolled around and around, combining with the shaking of the mountain until Rémy no longer had any idea whether she was on her feet or on her back.

Then: nothing.

The quake stopped. In the space of a whip-crack, the world went so still and so dark that Rémy thought she must be dead — dead and floating in the void between whatever comes between now and after.

Seconds that felt like hours stretched into the void as Rémy's hearing slowly returned. At first she thought she was surrounded by silence, but then she realized she could hear breathing — and not only her own.

"R-Rémy? Are you there? Are you all right?"

Thaddeus's voice floated to her out of the darkness. The sound of it flooded her with relief.

"I'm here." Rémy realized she was lying on her side, her cheek against the dirt floor. There was dust in her nose and her cheekbone throbbed with a dull ache — she must have cracked it against the rock as she fell. Coughing, she slowly sat upright, testing her body as she would if she had fallen from the wire. "I'm not hurt."

Beside her there was the sound of fabric scuffing against stone, then a groan that resolved itself into a cough.

"Kai?"

"I'm all right," he said.

There was more sound of movement as they all began to pull themselves upright.

"J?" asked a faint voice.

"Dita!" there came the sound of a match being struck, and flame flared in the darkness, illuminating J's eager face. It lasted a few seconds before dying. "Are you all right?"

"Yes," said the little girl, her voice barely above a whisper. "What — what happened? I — I cannot remember . . ."

"Don't you worry none about that for now," J soothed. There was the sound of tearing fabric, and then of another match being struck. The flame flared again as Rémy got to her feet, her eyes searching for Thaddeus. The light lasted longer this time — J had torn a strip from his shirt, setting fire to it.

Rémy reached Thaddeus as he got to his feet. She pulled him to her, and he tucked her head under his chin.

"Are you hurt?" she asked.

"No, just winded. Desai," Thaddeus asked, raising his voice and turning slightly to look at the older man, "is it over?"

Desai was looking past them with a frown, down the dark passageway through which they had fled. "Possibly. I suggest we keep moving, just in case."

"I agree," said the raja. "We should not wait around to find out."

"Well," Kai said, dragging himself to his feet though his leg was still bleeding. "The quake seems to be done with. I'm going back. Upala might still be alive."

"Don't be ridiculous," said Rémy, pushing herself out of Thaddeus's arms to turn to her brother. "You can't, Kai. Even if the Sapphire Cutlass is dead, not all of her followers will be."

Her brother gave her a steady look. "Then I'll take them on. Now that the ground's stopped shaking, it'll be easier. Besides, with their goddess gone, they will be leaderless."

"There's still Sahoj," said Thaddeus.

Kai made a disdainful sound in his throat. "That fat old man? He's nothing but flesh and blood. I'm not afraid of him." He pulled his sword free from its scabbard and turned, bracing himself uncertainly against the wall.

"Do not be so sure that the Sapphire Cutlass has been defeated," Desai said softly, his gaze still fixed over Kai's shoulders.

The pirate turned. "What? What are you saying?"

"That we really should go," the old man said softly. "Before we find out that Upala and her opal were not as strong as we hoped."

Kai's face convulsed at that. He gripped the hilt of his drawn sword so tightly that his knuckle glowed white against its golden tint. "With those words you prove what a fool you are, old man," said the pirate through gritted teeth. "Upala's spirit is stronger than that of any goddess."

Desai lifted his hands in appeasement. "I meant no disrespect. Upala has proven herself to be of brave heart and noble mind. No fault lies at her feet. I merely meant —"

A noise swelled out of the darkness, a cacophony of sound rolling along the tunnel toward them like a tidal wave. It was a piercing scream, made not just of one voice, but of many — a war cry, high and grating, full of abject fury and bile.

J pulled Dita against his side, wrapping his arms around her as a look of fear spread across his face. "What the bleedin' 'eck is that? Sounds like a ton of pigs havin' their necks cut wiv a razor blade."

A light appeared at the end of the tunnel, a blue glow that grew even as they watched it. Black shadows flickered at its heart, drawing closer and closer by the second as the light swelled ever brighter. By the time that any of them realized what they were seeing, the tide was almost upon them.

"We have failed!" Desai cried as the shadows solidified into the forms of the Sapphire Cutlass's foot soldiers, howling their insane fury as they charged. "Run. *RUN!*"

{Chapter 30}

A SAPPHIRE TIDE

$\mathcal{T}$he tide of running, thrashing fury was on them before they could move more than a few steps. Bodies surrounded them, a sea of armor spoiling for the final fight. Rémy found herself alone, marooned as Kai was torn away from her, buffeted by the eddies of an ocean that had once been human, but was now pure rage. Thaddeus and the others were drowning somewhere ahead of her, already out of view. Rémy found herself spun this way and that, turned and tumbled until even her legendary sense of equilibrium found it hopeless to tell which way was up.

A muscled, metaled hand clamped around her throat. Choking, she was drawn against the chest of a colossus whose vengeful eyes were rimmed with pure blue. His mouth screamed at her, the noise lost in the maelstrom's entirety. Rémy fought, gasping for breath, but he lifted her from the ground as if she were nothing more than a struggling bug.

Through the sound of dying blood rushing in her ears, Rémy became aware of something else. The blue glow had reached them too, along with a fusing, cracking sound. The bright sapphire hue washed along the passageway, coloring the stone — no, not just coloring it, changing it: turning it into pure gem. Electricity traced the air, sheer power dancing with the oxygen that she couldn't pull into her lungs. Around them, above them, below them — all was the pale, glittering blue of sapphire, moving past where Rémy fought for life, past where the supernatural army fought a battle they were sure to win.

The hand on Rémy's neck loosened. The rage in her attacker's eyes turned to fear. He dropped her and she fell to her knees in the dirt, hands grasping at her neck as she struggled to gulp great drafts of air into her lungs. Looking up, Rémy watched in fascinated horror as he began to clutch at his own chest. The sapphire embedded in his skin was vibrating as it glittered with a fierce glow.

Screaming, the soldier dropped to his knees. He would have crashed into Rémy if she hadn't scrambled backward. Around them, all the men and women of the Sapphire Cutlass were doing the same — screaming in fear and pain, writhing their armored fingers against their chests and arms — anywhere they had fastened a sapphire into their skin.

The stones were growing, transforming the human flesh around themselves from skin and fat and bone to rock-hard sapphire. Rémy saw it radiate from the tattoo, swallowing the black lines of the drawn cutlass as if it had never existed, opening up a transparency in the man's chest that looked like a void. He kept screaming until the gem's growth had spread to his throat, where his cry strangled and died. The last thing to go were his eyes, which looked at Rémy with a pitiful plea, as if the woman he had been trying to slaughter a second ago could somehow be his savior now. A moment later, there was nothing before her but a shape cut out of sapphire that had once been human.

Around her, the horror was being played out over and over again as the foot soldiers of the Sapphire Cutlass were turned to stone — not animated, moving stone as she had been, but dead, inert crystalline structures with no life apart from what glinted in them as light glanced from the unnatural angles of their surfaces.

Something grabbed her arm — Kai, who had battled through the dying cult members to her side. She couldn't hear what he was shouting at her over their horrible screams, but he waved one arm and she turned her head to see the others, urging them to run. The passageway, ahead and behind them, was now made of sapphire, and the stone was continuing to spread, turning what had once been the darkness ahead of them into a tunnel of prismatic blue light. The only part that had remained untouched was the dirt path beneath their feet, a gray ribbon leading them through the vivid blue.

Rémy, still stunned, found it difficult to move. Kai wrapped his arm around her waist and staggered forward, pulling her onward despite his own injury. Thaddeus must have seen her hesitate, because he passed Dita to Desai and started back toward them.

"Come on," he bellowed into her ear once he reached them, squeezing her arm with one hand. "We have to hurry."

Thaddeus hooked Kai's other arm over his shoulder and together they hoisted him up, carrying him between them.

"What's happening?" Rémy shouted, not even sure her voice could carry to Thaddeus's ears over the din. *Is this it?* she wondered. *Can the Sapphire Cutlass only destroy? Will the entire world turn to stone?*

Thaddeus hadn't heard her, but he was trying to tell them something anyway.

"Don't touch," he yelled. "Desai says, whatever you do, don't try to take one of the sapphires."

For once in her life, Rémy had absolutely no interest in owning a gemstone.

They ran, dodging transforming and transformed cult members, trying not to touch the human statues that littered their path. Rémy saw one such statue topple against another pure sapphire form as it fell, shattering into a cascade of smaller jewels. Kai, answering some kind of reflex, tried to bend to pick one up, but Rémy and Thaddeus stopped him.

Ahead of them, Rémy saw the raja do the same. He paused for a moment, as if mesmerized, before snatching up handfuls of sapphire. Desai realized what he was doing and tried to yell a warning, but it was too late.

The raja started to scream. He opened his palm and tried to shake the jewels from his hand, but they had already fused with his skin. They burrowed like insects into his very being, and in a second his veins were flooding with a blue light that tore through his body like fire. His hand became sapphire. The once-proud raja held it out to them as they passed, as if somehow one of them could do something to help him. The jewel spread up his arm to his shoulder, exploded into his chest, then rose up his neck to his gaping, screaming mouth. He fell silent, enveloped in stone.

The sound of the terror receded as they left those horrors behind them. The sapphire was still spreading — the rooms through which Upala and Rémy had crept with wonder were all now a uniform blue, simple and cold in its purity. They stumbled out of the entrance to the mountain and saw that both the statues and the carvings were all also transformed.

Rémy was relieved to see, though, that the sapphire had apparently reached the extent of its growth. The creepers that grew in elaborate tangles over the surface of the mountain temple were still alive, and still wore the green and tan hues of their true selves. The jungle outside was still there as well — brighter, lighter and greener, somehow, than it had been when they had first began their sojourn inside the mountain.

The group stumbled out into the open and collapsed a few paces away from the temple's entrance. Kai grunted with pain as he hit the ground. They all sprawled out on the warm earth, exhausted and gasping for breath.

"What in the name of blazes were that?" J rasped, Dita's hand clutched tightly in his. "I thought we were done for, good and proper!"

Desai began to laugh, a deep, rumbling sound that Rémy realized she'd never heard before.

"What's so funny?" J asked, irritated as he sat up.

The older man sat up, too, and reached out to clap J on the back. "My dear, dear J — I thought we were done for, too. I thought the Sapphire Cutlass had won." He looked over to Kai with a smile. "But it seems that Kai was right. I underestimated Upala's strength."

"You mean, what happened just then, that was the opal working?" Thaddeus asked, looking up at the pure sapphire of the mountain.

Desai followed his gaze. "I think it was more than that. My guess is that the power of the Sapphire Cutlass was actually too great for the opal to contain. The energy released — the power it tried to drain from her — had to be absorbed by something else. So the mountain took it back. The mountain reclaimed its power, and in doing so, finally regained what had been stolen from it, so many years ago."

"So that's it?" Kai asked. "It's all over?"

Desai nodded, his exhaustion beginning to show on his face. "That would be my hope, yes."

"You can't be sure?"

The older man lifted his palms in a humble shrug. "One can never be sure."

Silence fell around them as they all contemplated Desai's words. In it, somewhere in the depths of the jungle valley, a bird sang a happy song.

"Listen to that," said Thaddeus, raising his head and shutting his eyes under the sun's golden rays. "There were no birds here before we went in to the mountain. The valley seems different. It *feels* different. More . . . alive, somehow."

"Well," said Desai, "nature has a way of reasserting herself over man's folly."

"Can I go back in?" Kai asked. "I need . . . I need to find Upala."

Rémy felt her heart twinge in sympathy. She laid a hand on his arm. "Kai . . . I don't think there is any hope that she —"

"I know," Kai cut her off gruffly, looking at his feet. "She's dead. I know that. But . . . I feel like I have to see her. I have to . . . pay my last respects."

Rémy looked at Desai, who seemed troubled.

"Would it be safe?" she asked. "The earthquake has gone. There doesn't seem to be any more . . . transformations happening. Is it over?"

Desai paused before answering. "I think it would be prudent to wait. I really have no way of knowing what is happening inside the mountain. Wait, Kai, until the morning. Until you have rested and I have seen to the wound in your leg. I think . . . that Upala can wait for you."

Kai nodded. Rémy watched her brother's face for a moment, until she saw that his eyes were filling with tears. Then she turned away.

★ ★ ★

They collected wood for a fire as the shadows lengthened in the valley, turning the sky overhead from azure to indigo before eventually fading into darkness completely. Thaddeus helped J and Rémy gather the wood, reflecting silently on the events of the past few days. The valley's natural life was, as Desai had said, reasserting itself. Night creatures crept around them, skittering in the undergrowth, which itself seemed lighter somehow. Of the mist that had concealed their attackers, there was no sign.

Thaddeus watched Rémy. They hadn't spoken

much yet, besides holding each other close in a brief reassurance that they were indeed both still whole. There had been a moment there, when he'd left her on top of Dita's cage surrounded by hundreds of murderous acolytes, that Thaddeus had really thought he might never see her again. He wondered what it meant that he'd left anyway. Kai had wanted to stay with Upala, even though he knew it would have been hopeless.

Thaddeus hadn't wanted to leave Rémy there. Of course he hadn't. It was just that they had spent so long weathering such dangers together that he knew how she would have reacted if he hadn't gone to help Desai instead of staying with her. She wouldn't have thanked him for it. She probably would have resorted to one of the old insults she used to use back before they were together, in London, and called him stupid. It wasn't that Rémy didn't need protecting. Everyone needed protecting in one way or another. It was just that she wouldn't allow it. And he loved her. What was love if it wasn't accepting what the person you loved wanted, even if it wasn't what you would choose for yourself?

They built the fire and lit it, settling around it quietly as it crackled and sparked in the dark. Thaddeus found himself staring quietly at the flames, sitting with his elbows on his knees as Desai fixed up Kai's leg with Rémy's help.

"Penny for them?" she asked, coming to sit beside him a few minutes later, close enough to lean her head against his tired shoulder.

Thaddeus turned and kissed the top of her head. "Just . . . taking it all in, I suppose. What happened back there . . . it could easily have been the end of the world, which is just . . . staggering, really."

Rémy pressed herself closer to him and he sat back, wrapping one arm around her shoulders to pull her against his chest.

"We couldn't have done it without Upala and Kai," she said, quiet enough that her voice would not carry over the flames. "He is so upset, Thaddeus. He's trying to hide it, but . . . I think he's heartbroken."

Thaddeus buried his nose in her hair and looked over the flames to her twin. Kai held his bandaged leg stiffly out in front of him, staring into the middle distance as if he didn't see any of it at all. *There but for the grace of God go I*, Thaddeus thought to himself. *If I lost Rémy now . . .* He pushed the thought away and shut his eyes for a moment, feeling the rise and fall of her breathing as they sat twined together, almost as close as it was possible for two humans to be. It seemed impossible to imagine that they didn't belong exactly as they were now.

"He's determined to go back into the mountain," Rémy continued quietly, oblivious to Thaddeus's train of thought.

"I suppose there's nothing we can do to stop him," Thaddeus murmured.

"No, there isn't. So I am going to go too."

Thaddeus felt a sick twist of worry knot itself into his stomach. "Rémy, no — we don't know what you'll find in there. We don't know for sure if its safe. We don't even know —"

She pulled gently out of his arms and straightened up to face him. "Thaddeus, I can't let him go alone. He is my brother — my true twin. I've only known him a few days. I can't leave him to do something like this alone now. Especially not when it's my fault that —"

Thaddeus moved to cup her face in both his hands. "It's not your fault."

"If I hadn't gone to find them — if I hadn't convinced them to help us, then . . ."

"It is not your fault, Rémy Brunel. I won't allow you to think that. It's Sahoj's fault, it's the raja's fault, it's Aruna's fault . . . I don't know, it's that legendary

Portuguese man who lived hundreds of years ago's fault. But it is not yours, no matter what you might think."

Rémy's lips curved in a watery smile. "You are too nice to me, Englishman."

Thaddeus kissed her gently, warmly. "You deserve it." He pulled her to him again, settling her head against his chest. "You're still going to go, though, aren't you?"

Rémy tightened her arms around him. "I have to. Does that make you hate me?"

Thaddeus laughed quietly. "Of course I don't hate you. I love you, Rémy Brunel. I always will, no matter what crazy, harebrained situations you drag me into. Don't you know that by now?"

Chapter 31

OPALS AND BONES

The mountain stayed silent all night, no unpleasant echoes of the events that had taken place in its depths drifting out of its transformed mouth. In the morning a new sun rose over the valley, casting its rays against the biggest sapphire Rémy had ever seen. She stood, her feet damp with early-morning dew, and watched as the dawn light refracted against the ancient carvings, now as blue as the sky over her head. The jewel itself, though, seemed quieter, somehow, as if whatever peculiar electricity had animated it had gone.

"Ready?" Kai asked, stepping to her side. He was still limping, but his stride was stronger than it had been the night before. Behind them stood the others:

Desai, J, Dita, and Thaddeus, waiting for them to set off back into the mountain.

"Yes," she told him. "Are you?"

Kai looked up at the mountain, squinting in the already-bright sunlight, his face impassive. "As ready as I will ever be, little sister. Let's go."

He moved off, his pace slow to accommodate his injured leg. Rémy hung back, turning to Thaddeus with a smile. He walked toward her, leaning down to kiss her gently.

"Don't be long," he said softly.

She kissed him back. "We won't be. Don't get sunburned while I'm gone."

Thaddeus smiled and let her go. Rémy followed Kai, up the sapphire steps, through the great archway, and into the mountain.

The sunlight, so bright outside, faded away once they had gone just a little way. They had been prepared for that, bringing torches that had been wrapped with cloth donated from their clothes. Whatever happened next, once all this was done, Rémy told herself, they would all need new suits of clothes. It was amazing that the ones they had still held together, they were so tattered. She thought of the silks and embroidered drapes that adorned the inner chambers of the raja's palace, and wondered what the chances were of being able to get hold of them. Slim, most likely. She couldn't imagine that, in the absence of both the raja and Sahoj, the place hadn't already been ransacked, and she couldn't blame the people for doing that. They deserved to take back what had been taken from them for so long.

With a torch each, it was easier to see the way. The flame-light haloed against the sapphire walls, reflecting back over and over until it seemed as if they were walking through a hall of mirrors. There was no sign of movement, save for them. The stone was as dead as the cult members they came across — or rather, what was left of the cult members, who remained where they had been standing when the transformation overcame them, frozen for all eternity in twisted, ice-cold sapphire versions of themselves.

Rémy tried not to touch anything. The stone seemed to be dead, but after witnessing what had happened to all these people — not to mention to the raja, whose transparent, invaluable carcass they passed — she was in no hurry to test the theory.

At length they passed into the cavern. Their torches were not strong enough to light the entire space and flickered and died beyond a circle around them both.

But it was enough to illuminate more bodies of pure jewel, all caught in poses of flight as they had tried to outrun the explosion of power behind them.

"The torches on the walls," Kai whispered, sending sibilant echoes into the dark void that answered back, over and over again. "We should light them."

"Will they not have been turned to sapphire too?" Rémy asked, disturbed by the echo of her own voice rolling around them.

Rémy's supposition was right. Every fixture, from the wooden shaft of each torch to the metal rivets that had held them in place, had been transformed into gemstone. There was nothing for it but for them to feel their way, slowly, with the light they had.

As they walked deeper into the cavern, they came across more and more sapphire corpses. In some places, they were so close together that it was almost impossible to find a way through. Their limbs tangled together like a climbing rose bush, so impenetrable that at last Kai, frustrated, drew his sword and before Rémy could raise her voice to stop him, had smashed it down, cutting through a mess of crystalline arms and legs.

Rémy froze as the gems shattered, listening with a pounding heart as the broken stones tinkled against the sapphire floor. She was convinced that something would come rushing at them from the jagged dark beyond their torchlights — something ravenous with anger. But there was nothing but the echoes of the skittering gems. Kai pushed onward through the path he had made as a new feeling of misgiving flooded through Rémy.

"Kai — wait," she urged, ignoring the incessant echoes of her own words. "Please. Listen to me, just for a moment."

Her brother turned to face her, his weather-beaten face taking on the reflections of blue stone and orange flame.

"I just . . ." Rémy took a breath, wondering how to say what was worrying her. "It's Upala. Kai, the same thing has happened to everything inside this place. Everything. Upala — she's going to look just like this now. She is going to *be* just like this. Do you really need to see that? Don't you want to . . . remember her as she was, not as she is now?"

Kai glanced around him at the carcasses of the cult. He took a breath, a look of unutterable sadness fleetingly crossing his features. It was gone in an instant, replaced by a clenched jaw and a familiar look of determination.

"I have to find her," he said. "I have to."

Rémy looked at him for another second, and then nodded. They moved on, past the pit of snakes that no longer writhed but instead were frozen in permanent curlicues. They forced their way between more death, and finally up onto the stone stage. Rémy could see the tension radiating from Kai's shoulders, knowing that Upala must be somewhere close. He stalked forward, his limp almost indistinguishable beneath the forceful movement of his steps.

He stopped.

"Rémy," he said, his voice thick — and remarkably, there was no echo. *"Look."*

She moved to her brother's side and looked up at what he had found. Rémy drew in a sharp, amazed breath.

In front of them was the throne of the Sapphire Cutlass. In it was seated Aruna, the girl-goddess who had turned against the world itself. She was slumped backward, arms outstretched along her arm rests, eyes closed as if she were merely asleep — and she was flesh and blood.

Gone was the taint of sapphire that had so poisoned her body, gone was the pure blue transparency of her legs and arms. Instead there was only burnished skin, as human and as fallible as that of Rémy's own.

"I . . . don't understand . . ." Rémy muttered, awestruck.

Then Kai moved his torch, lifting it to his left. Beside the throne was a pillar of pure sapphire — not formed in the shape of anything but itself, a large tablet of glittering jewel. Inside was the perfectly preserved form of Upala. She stood as if on tiptoe, arms by her side, head raised and eyes open. She looked as fierce and beautiful as ever, and so unharmed that at first Rémy thought she was still alive. But there was no rise and fall in her breast and no space for air between the limits of her being and the sapphire that surrounded her. She was dead. Beautiful, eternal — but dead.

Kai stepped up to the pillar, dropped his sword, and slumped to his knees before Upala's magnificent tomb. Rémy could see tears running down his face, and it was clear that for now, he did not care if she saw them. He stood there, silently looking up at Upala for a long time. Rémy looked away, wanting to give them privacy, somehow. Her eye was caught by something lying on the ground. She stooped to pick it up, recognizing it at once.

"Kai," she said gently, holding it out to him.

It was a pendant fashioned from opal, hanging on a gold chain. Within the opal's milky whiteness shone a thick band of iridescent blue. Kai took it from her and coiled the necklace in his palm as a tear fell from his face to glide across the stone's surface. He passed his thumb across it.

"She always wanted to know where it came from," Kai muttered thickly, staring at the gem in his hand. "The opal, I mean. She knew it wasn't from anywhere on this continent. I told her, it was from Australasia — so far away and so dangerous a place that it's where the British send their criminals. She wanted to go, and I told her . . ." he trailed off, and then started again. "I told her that one day, we'd go. One day, I'd sail her all the way there, just because she wanted to go. I thought that was as good as telling her I loved her. But it wasn't. I loved her, and I never told her. Why didn't I *tell* her?"

Rémy put a hand on his arm. "She knew, Kai. And she loved you, too. You knew that, didn't you?"

Kai looked up at Upala, suspended forever in her magnificent jewel. "It's not the same," he said, his voice cracking. "Life's too short, little sister. Life's too short not to say what you mean."

Rémy wrapped her arms around her brother. After

a moment, he held her, too. Two lost twins, finally reunited.

At length Kai gave a big sniff and pulled away. "We should go," he said. "There's nothing more we can do here."

Rémy nodded, and then looked at Aruna's curiously unmarred human corpse. "What should we do with her?" she asked.

Kai gave the body a long look. "Leave her there," he said. "Her bones belong to the mountain. Let it keep them."

Epilogue

"You know what would be really useful right now?" said J as they made the journey out of the valley. "An airship. Didn't we have one once? Oh, yeah — we did. And someone crashed it."

"I did *not* crash it, J," Rémy sighed. "We were hit by a flaming arrow."

"Yeah," grumbled J, "an' *then* you crashed."

"Hush," said Dita, who was walking beside him. Desai was a little way ahead of them, leading the way. "The walk will do us good."

"Hrumph," J muttered. "What we just went through, we need sleep, not bleedin' exercise."

"Oh, yes, I was forgetting," said Dita, her voice caustic, "what a hard time you had back there, dirty boy. All that running around was terrible, yes? Far worse than getting bitten by a snake and being turned into a monster."

"I *ain't* dirty, an' that wasn't what I meant," J protested. "And you wasn't a monster! Not even close!"

"What was I then?" Dita asked, slipping her hand into his. "A freak? Like one of those poor beardy women you see in a circus?"

"Bearded women," J corrected. "And no, you wasn't a freak, neither."

They carried on bickering as they walked, their chatter fading into the background with the chirrup of the crickets as Thaddeus tuned them out. They had been walking for a long while already, and it would be longer still before they reached the valley's edge and moved out of the mountain's shadow. Thaddeus was tired, but happy — relieved to be leaving this place behind, and also at Rémy's reports of what had happened inside. That Upala was truly dead was a tragedy, for sure, but knowing that the rest of the cult had been similarly subdued was cause for relief.

Thaddeus became aware that Rémy was no longer at his side. He turned to see that she had dropped back, putting space between herself and the rest of the group. Thaddeus slowed his pace, falling into step with her.

"Everything all right?" he asked, anxious when he saw the thoughtful look on her face. "What's the matter?"

"Nothing's the matter. I've just been thinking, that is all."

"Oh? What about?" Thaddeus glanced up the slight hill they were climbing to where her brother Kai soldiered onward, stoic despite his grief and pain. No doubt Rémy was thinking about him. What must it have been like, to think you were alone in the world and then to come face-to-face with your twin? It must have been —

"Will you marry me?" Rémy asked.

Thaddeus stopped dead in his tracks, looking at her in astonishment. "What?"

Rémy stopped beside him and shrugged. "I've been thinking about it for a while, but . . . something that Kai said, back there, made me realize that I should just go ahead and ask," she said. "So do you want to? Get married, I mean?"

Something fierce and hot radiated out from Thaddeus's heart as he caught her arm and pulled her to him. "Do I *want* to? Rémy — of course I want to! But I thought — I wasn't sure that you . . ." He took a breath and willed his heart to calm down as he stepped back and looked at her, smiling widely. "Rémy Brunel.

Nothing would make me happier than to be your husband, and to call you my wife. In fact . . ."

"What is it?" Rémy asked, puzzled as he pulled away and reached for one of the pockets in his trousers.

Thaddeus found what he was looking for. Pulling out a small twist of paper, he unwrapped a small ring. It had been formed of two thin bands of gold, twisted together in a wreath to hold a tiny diamond. He hesitated for a moment, and then reached out to take Rémy's left hand. He looked at her face and saw the delight spreading across the features that he had come to love so well. Smiling, he slipped the ring onto her finger. It fit perfectly.

"I know it's only tiny, but I thought," he said quietly, "that you deserved to have a diamond that you didn't have to steal."

Rémy stared at the ring, holding it up so the little stone could catch the light. "It's beautiful," she whispered. Then she cast him a look. "How long have you had this in your pocket?" she demanded. "And where did you get it from?"

"Ahh," said Thaddeus, holding up both hands. "That would be telling. I've got to have *some* secrets."

Rémy grabbed his hands, laughing. "What, even as my husband?"

Thaddeus laughed with her, wrapping her up in his arms and kissing her soundly. "Well, perhaps not *then* . . ."

"Why did you never ask me?" Rémy said. "If you had the ring . . ."

Thaddeus shrugged. "I could never work out how."

Rémy rested her forehead against his. "I find that simply usually works."

"Yes," Thaddeus laughed. "Apparently so."

"The only thing is," Rémy added, "I am not sure I could ever be 'Rémy Rec.' It just doesn't . . ." she trailed off with a grimace.

Thaddeus made a face. "Ugh. No, I can see what you mean. I'm not sure you could ever be anything other than Rémy Brunel anyway. Maybe I should take your name instead."

Rémy looked up at him. "Really?"

Thaddeus shrugged. "Why not? Thaddeus Brunel has a bit of a ring to it, don't you think?"

Rémy raised her eyebrows. "It's a very French name. I am not sure you could be sufficiently French to own it. For a start you would have to drink less tea."

"Oh, god." Thaddeus stopped, a look of mock horror on his face. "I can't do it, Rémy. I love you, but I just can't."

She punched him lightly in the arm as they both laughed. "Stupid man."

"What are you two laughing about?" asked a voice.

It was Kai, watching them with a slight, subdued smile. Thaddeus and Rémy parted, still holding hands. Thaddeus saw Kai's gaze drop to the little ring on Rémy's finger.

"Ahh," he said with a smile that managed to be both wider and sadder at the same time. "I see that congratulations are in order."

"Kai, I am sorry," Rémy said, faltering over the words. "I know — I know that you . . . that you . . ."

Kai stepped forward and grasped his sister's hand. "There is no need to be sorry for anything, little sister," he said softly. "I am glad that you have more sense than me — in some things, any way. I am very happy for you both."

Rémy let go of Thaddeus to hug her brother fiercely. "Thank you, brother. That means much to me."

When they parted, Rémy took Thaddeus's hand again and the three of them started to walk, following the others once more.

"So," Kai asked, "what are you two going to do now? Besides tying the knot, I mean. Will you go back to England?"

Thaddeus glanced at Rémy, who looked back with a shrug. It was a good question, and one that neither of them had considered at all.

"There's not much for me in England," Thaddeus admitted. "They'll never make me a policeman again."

"Are you sure?" Rémy asked, looking up at him with concern etched on her brow. "You were the best they had, Thaddeus. You might be surprised — I bet they would be glad to have you back."

"I doubt it," he sighed. "Besides, after all the things we've seen, all the places we've been, knowing what else is out there in the world . . . Well, I'm not sure I want to go back, really. What about you, Rémy? It's not just about what I want — what do you want to do next?"

Rémy's gaze drifted toward her brother. "I don't know," she said, "although I would like a chance to get to know the only family I have . . ."

Kai gave her a smile, and then a smirk. "Well," he said slowly. "You know, I do have need of more good hands aboard my ship. I always told Upala that if she left me, I'd have to find two to replace her. I wasn't lying." He shrugged. "You could join my crew. I'd be glad to have you — both of you."

Thaddeus grimaced in answer to Rémy's raised

eyebrows. "Look . . . I may not be a policeman any-more . . . but I don't think I could be a pirate."

"Really?" Rémy teased. "And there I was thinking you were looking quite piratical these days, what with your torn shirts and your constant tan."

Thaddeus laughed, squeezing her hand. "I'm sorry, Rémy, but I couldn't."

She smiled at him softly. "I know. You're just too good a man for thievery and plunder, whatever the cause. I'm sorry, Kai," she said, addressing her brother, "but I think we have to say no."

Kai nodded with a grin. "I expected as much. Pity. Although . . ." He trailed off, looking thoughtful.

"What?" Rémy asked.

Kai shrugged. "I think I might be over the pirate life too, at least for now. I have another ship — smaller than the *Black Star*, but just as sea-worthy. The *Silver Cygnet*. I could take her and sail anywhere I wanted to — as long as I had a crew to help me, of course."

"A crew?" Thaddeus asked. "How big of a crew?"

"Not many. Four should do it, with me besides." Kai's gaze drifted ahead to where J and Dita were still bickering merrily as they walked along, their feet kicking up trails of dust that flurried in their wake.

Rémy frowned. "And where were you thinking of taking this ship of yours?" she asked.

"I've not decided yet," Kai said quietly. Then he pulled Upala's opal from his pocket and held it up so that it swung in front of him. "Perhaps I will simply trust the wind to take me wherever it wishes to go."

Thaddeus looked down at Rémy, who looked back with a question on her face. He felt like laughing, and wondered how it could be that since he'd met her, life didn't seem to have even taken a breath, let alone stood still.

"What do you think Dita and J want to do next?" she asked him.

Thaddeus raised her fingers to his lips and kissed them. "I don't know," he said. "Let's ask them and find out."

ABOUT THE AUTHOR

$\mathscr{S}$haron Gosling always wanted to be a writer. She started as an entertainment journalist, writing about television series such as *Stargate* and *Battlestar Galactica*. Her first novel was published under a pen name in 2010. Sharon and her husband live in a very small cottage in a very remote village in the north of England, surrounded by sheep-dotted fells. The village has its own vampire, although Sharon hasn't met it yet. The cat might have, but he seems to have been sworn to secrecy and won't say a thing.

ACKNOWLEDGEMENTS

The author would like to thank editors Penny West and Abby Huff, and Liam Peters and Kay Fraser for creating the cover. Thanks also to Adam for unerring support and, as always, thanks to the readers!